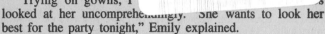

"Where is your sister?" [...] bled through the garden, [...]

"Trying on gowns, I [...] looked at her uncomprehendingly. She wants to look her best for the party tonight," Emily explained.

"And she needs all day to do that?"

Emily considered. "Yes, I believe she does."

Charles made a sound of disgust.

"Come now," teased Emily. "You aren't going to tell me you don't spend a great deal of time in choosing a waistcoat or in tying a cravat."

"Of course I spend a great deal of time," agreed Charles. "But it don't take me all afternoon."

"You are not a great beauty with a reputation to maintain," pointed out Emily.

"Well, thank God I am not," said Charles heartily. "And thank God you don't consider yourself one, either, Emily, for who should I have to talk with if you were like Elyza and holed up in your room all day?"

Emily sighed. "No, there is no danger of me considering myself a great beauty," she said wistfully.

Charles looked at her, and seeing the sadness in her eyes, said, "You shouldn't let it blue devil you that you ain't as pretty as your sister."

"Oh, it doesn't bother me so very much," said Emily, trying to sound cheerful. "After all, we cannot all be beautiful. Although sometimes I wonder why."

Charles laughed at this. "I can tell you why," he said. "If we were all as beautiful as your sister, we should all spend the day in our rooms, prancing before the looking glass, seeing no one and doing nothing, and that would be the devil of a bore!"

Emily found it impossible to hold down a smile.

"Emily! You have a dimple," observed Charles in amazement. Emily blushed scarlet, but he didn't notice, so caught up was he in digesting this new discovery. "I wonder I never noticed it before," he said and shook his head. "I rather like dimples . . ."

ZEBRA'S REGENCY ROMANCES
DAZZLE AND DELIGHT

The Accidental Bride

Sheila Rabe

ZEBRA BOOKS
KENSINGTON PUBLISHING CORP.

To Louise, who knows the meaning
of "Pretty is as Pretty does."

ZEBRA BOOKS are published by

Kensington Publishing Corp.
850 Third Avenue
New York, NY 10022

Zebra and the Z logo Reg. U.S. Pat. & TM Off.

First Printing: June, 1994

Printed in the United States of America

Chapter One

Emily Vane sighed as her maid tried to coax her limp locks into fashionable curls. Sometimes life seemed so unfair.

Elyza's hair was the same color, but her curls never fell limp, even after an entire night of dancing. Even at her most dishevelled, Elyza was undisguisedly beautiful.

"Oh, you look lovely, Miss Emily," Foster rhapsodized, patting a curl. "I think this is the most flattering style we have tried yet."

Emily looked at her reflection and was pleasantly surprised. For four guineas the curled headdress had been an excellent investment. "It is quite nice," she told her maid. Turning her head, Emily admired the way the false hair blended with her own. "I do believe this style makes my cheeks look thinner."

Foster nodded enthusiastically and pinned a lock into place. "Yes, and I think it shows up your fine brown eyes, too."

Emily smiled. Then the door opened and her stepsister entered, a golden-haired vision in a muslin gown of palest pink. Emily's smile faded. Why couldn't she have had blue eyes? "Hullo Elyza," she said in depressed tones.

Elyza glided into the room. She stood next to Emily and examined the new hairstyle. "That is quite flattering," she finally admitted. "However, it will never stay. One set of country dances and it will all be in your face. The part that is really yours, that is."

Emily scowled at her insolent stepsister. "I shall try it, anyway," she announced.

Elyza shrugged. It obviously made no difference to her whether or not Emily tried a new hairstyle.

Emily suspected that, when it came right down to it, it made little difference to her, too. For it wasn't her hair that was her undoing. It was her face.

It was not a repulsive face. But it was, unfortunately, rather plain. Her brown eyes were nice. But her nose was too short, her lips too large, and her face, instead of a lovely aristocratic oval, was too round. Peasant round, Elyza would tease spitefully when the sisters quarrelled. Emily was often described as kind. Or sweet. Alas, never beautiful.

Elyza's face was also rarely described as beautiful. Words like perfect and breathtaking were more often used. And the descriptions were accurate. Elyza's face was as perfect as her figure. Even her manners—when in public—were perfect. Emily sighed.

"Run along, Foster," Elyza was saying. "I want to talk to Emily."

"Yes, Miss," said Foster. "Let me just pin this one last curl."

Elyza pinched Foster's arm and the woman let out a yelp. "Go on, you wicked creature. I want to talk to Emily alone. And now, not when it suits you."

Foster fled the room, and Emily turned on her stepsister. "That was a mean, cruel thing to do, and I'll thank you to allow me to handle my own maid."

"You do not handle her at all," said Elyza scornfully. "She is far too uppity, and if you do not stop being such a milksop and start teaching her some manners, I shall have Mama turn her off."

"If you have come to ask to borrow something, this is hardly the way to begin," Emily observed.

Elyza gave her sister a sly look. "No," she said. "I have not come to ask for anything. I have come to offer you something."

Emily looked suspiciously at her. Elyza rarely offered anything unless it came with strings attached. "You are feeling gracious this morning, little sister?"

Elyza flopped onto Emily's bed. "How would you like to dance every dance at the masked ball tomorrow night?"

"I shouldn't like it at all," said Emily flippantly. "My curls would go limp, and I should look a wreck."

"Come now, Em. I am being serious. I have a plan."

"Which means you want to do something of which Mama would disapprove," translated Emily.

"Em," said Elyza in pleading tones. "Don't be such a spoil sport. Anyway, aren't you even the least bit curious to know what my plan is?"

"Oh, tell it to me. I can see you are determined to do so no matter what I wish."

"Very well," said Elyza happily. "It has to do with Lady Selwyn's masked ball."

"Oh, dear," murmured Emily.

Elyza ignored this and launched into an animated discourse.

Emily's eyes widened in disbelief as her sister talked. Elyza's plan was simple. Shortly after the ball had begun, she and Emily would change costumes and, thereby, identities for the evening. The advantages were many. "You shall most likely dance every dance, as I have already allowed several gentlemen to learn the secret of what I will be wearing. And you may flirt to your heart's content. Say and do what you will. I shall bear the consequences."

"What are you planning to do?" asked Emily suspiciously.

"Nothing disgraceful, I assure you. I merely wish to have an evening free from Mama's prying eyes."

"And why this sudden wish for freedom?" wondered Emily aloud. "It wouldn't have anything to do with a certain someone of whom Mama disapproves, would it?"

Elyza tossed her head. "And what if it does?"

"Oh, Elyza. You are treading on dangerous ground. You know Beddington is a rake."

"Even rakes must settle down sometime and set up their nurseries," said Elyza. "He is by far the handsomest of the men who are interested in me, and an earl to boot."

"Yes," said Emily scornfully. "And aptly titled, from what one hears. He'll ruin your reputation if you are not careful. The very fact he is an earl is why he won't look to you when he is ready to marry. He will expect to marry an heiress, or at least someone from a titled family."

"Stuff!" scoffed Elyza.

Emily frowned. There was obviously no talking any sense into her stepsister. Emily's stepmama had filled the girl's head with dreams of glory. The triumph of the famous Gunning sisters had been recounted many times, and Elyza rested secure in the knowledge that she was every bit as beautiful as they had been. Had not Mama told her so? If the Gunning sisters could come to town with nothing but their good looks to recommend them and marry well, so could Elyza Vane.

Emily wondered if the Gunning sisters had had to work as hard gaining an entrance to society as the Vane sisters. The *ton* seemed to have closed rank even more tightly since the Gunningses' triumph, and Mrs. Vane had been at great pains even to place her family at its fringes.

Money and comfort had been the best Harriett Vane could hope for when she married her first husband. Having accomplished that, when she again found herself free, the attractive young widow looked for social position. Mr. Vane, a quiet young widower whose father, it was rumored, was soon to be knighted, was the highest she could reach at the time. But he had seemed a wise choice. Surely, if his papa was about to be knighted, Mr. Vane must enjoy a properly lofty social position.

To her disappointment, Mrs. Vane discovered after her marriage that Mr. Vane did not enjoy a properly lofty social position at all and had no desire to do so. He was happy being a nobody, existing on the edges of the *ton*. He enjoyed his books, fine wine, good conversation, and he was perfectly content with his small collection of unimpressive friends. And to make matters worse, his papa never was knighted.

As time passed, leaving her in obscurity, Mrs. Vane despaired of ever becoming a part of that uppermost society in which she knew she belonged. And while her husband remained unconcerned, she watched her daughter grow into a beautiful young woman and wondered often and vociferously whatever was to become of the girls.

Just when she was about to give up, fortune smiled

on Mrs. Vane. Her second cousin, Lucy, after years of sitting on the shelf, married Lord James Runcible, a viscount, and became Lady Runcible. Here, at last, was Mrs. Vane's passport into the world of the Upper Ten Thousand.

Lady Runcible and Mrs. Vane had never been close as children and had been rivals as girls. But blood is thicker than water—so said Mrs. Vane—and after a little pleading and some emotional blackmail, a letter had been received from Lady Runcible giving her cousin the nebulous promise that she would do what she could.

On the strength of this letter, Mrs. Vane had moved her family to London and taken a house for the season. She had spent the first half of that season angling to gain vouchers for Almack's.

And even after that major hurdle had been gotten over, invitations to the various affairs of high society had trickled in slowly. Most of the ladies of the *ton* were not anxious to introduce a presumptuous nobody into their midst, especially a presumptuous nobody with a gorgeous young daughter who would attract the attention of the best matrimonial prizes.

But Mrs. Vane fought on, gleefully accepting any and all invitations which came her way, assuring her daughters with each new opportunity that, "Now we are getting somewhere."

Emily was sure they were, indeed, getting somewhere, but her stepmama did not have to tell her that their footing on the social ladder was still quite shaky. If Elyza took a misstep, it would spell social ruin for them all. And Emily suspected any step in the direction of furthering relations with the dissolute Lord Beddington was bound to be a misstep. "I don't know if this is such a good idea," she said hesitantly.

"Oh, don't be such a pudding heart," said Elyza. "What can it hurt?"

It was a tempting offer. Emily could dance at the ball disguised as her beautiful sister and be guaranteed a wonderful time. Perhaps, like Cinderella, she would meet her Prince Charming.

As her own plain self, Emily had few enough princes trailing after her. Of course, the young men she had met had been kind enough to her, but usually they only wanted to be with her so they could pump her for information about her stepsister. What was her sister's favorite flower? Was she fond of poetry? Did she seem to fancy one of her many suitors above the other? When were the ladies planning to go walking in the park next?

The only men who seemed to like Emily for herself were a middle-aged baronet, whose breath smelled like rotting teeth, and a bashful, pimply faced youth. Emily realized that beggars couldn't be choosers, but if those two were the only fashionable London beaus she was to be allowed to choose from, she would rather not choose at all. What would it be like to have as many suitors as her sister?

"Well?" prompted Elyza, returning Emily to the subject at hand.

"You are not going to do anything scandalous?"

Elyza was insulted. "Of course not. What kind of a goose do you think I am?"

Still Emily hesitated. "I shall be the one who is scolded if Mama learns of this," she predicted.

"No you won't."

Emily could almost hear her stepmama's words already. "You are the oldest. How could you have let your sister do something so foolish?" She was only a year older than Elyza, but a year's difference was obviously all that was necessary when one needed a scapegoat.

"Just think of what fun you will have disguised as me," said Elyza. "And I will let you have any presents that should happen to come for me the next day."

"Perhaps I shall keep some of your beaus," warned Emily. Elyza found this highly amusing. "There is no need to go into the whoops," Emily said stiffly as her sister's laughter danced about the room.

Elyza composed herself with great effort. "Well, what do you say?"

"Oh, all right," sighed Emily. "I suppose you will pester me to death if I don't give in."

With a squeal of delight, Elyza jumped from the bed and hugged her sister. "Oh, Em darling. I knew you would not let me down."

Perhaps I should have, thought Emily, already regretting her words. This is such a crazy scheme. Something is bound to happen. How could I have let Elyza talk me into this?

But deep down she knew the answer to that. Elyza's wild scheme would add an extra fillip to her life that would not otherwise be there. Elyza was spoiled, and she could be devious. But there was one thing Elyza was not, and that was dull. Emily suspected she would end up paying for this escapade. But as pleasant visions danced across her mind, she assured herself that no price would be too high.

"Here is what we shall do," Elyza was saying. "We will meet by the door after the first four dances. I will say I need to pin up my flounce, and you offer to help me. Once we are safely out of sight we will exchange costumes. I will don your domino and bird of paradise headdress, and you may wear my shepherdess costume.

We are of the same height, and with my mask and that bonnet to cover your face who will guess the difference?"

"But what of our gowns?" worried Emily. "We don't have gowns the same."

"I am wearing my peach colored one. Your pale pink one with the flounces is very much like it. In the candlelight who will be able to see clearly under a domino or a shawl?"

Emily trembled. It all seemed so very bold. She had heard about masked balls. Sometimes people behaved scandalously. It had seemed daring enough to her that they should even attend one. Now to go to such an affair as another person—goodness!

"It will be fine," Elyza assured her, as if reading her stepsister's mind.

And once at the ball the next night, Emily began to feel Elyza might, indeed, be right. For the costumes and masks and dominos made all the guests strangers.

Oh, some of the people were recognizable. The plump form and waddling gait of Emily's most ardent admirer, the baronet, was unmistakeable. And she was sure she recognized the honorable Mr. Sydney, her sister's tallest suitor.

But the other guests, once rendered faceless, had truly become nameless to her. Of course, she reminded herself, I know few of these people, anyway. Another favorable circumstance for two young ladies planning deception.

Two of the nameless throng watched as the Vane sisters entered the ballroom in their mama's wake. "There she is," said one, and both men sighed, their eyes following the young woman in the shepherdess costume.

"Perhaps tonight," said the other, "I shall be able to corner Miss Vane for a dance."

"You are not the only one who has penetrated her disguise, old fellow," said his friend.

The Honorable Charles Trevor, oldest son of Viscount Fairwood, MP, merely smiled confidently. "I'll wager the secret of Miss Vane's costume has not yet reached all her suitors' ears, for surely anyone with such valuable information would be in no hurry to share it. Indeed, I had to pay dearly for my knowledge."

Charles's friend, The Honorable Frederick Merriweather, acknowledged this wisdom. "You may be lucky. But you know you are playing against the odds. Johnston and Harn as well as old Mert have all been before you and have had a chance to further their acquaintance with the lady before you even got the opportunity to meet her."

"Yes, but tonight is my chance to steal a march on them," said Charles. "And I intend to. Excuse me, old fellow."

He left his friend and headed with determination in the direction of the three ladies, his goal the shepherdess hiding her lovely face behind the mask.

Alas, he arrived too late. A short, stout pirate beat him to her and led her onto the dance floor. Charles stopped short and backed away. He could have begged a dance from the girl in the pale green domino and the bird of paradise headdress, but he had seen both sisters, and he had no desire to dance with the older Miss Vane. Like his friends, Charles sought the diamond of the first water, with whom he'd already fallen in love. He placed himself against a wall and waited, hoping for a later opportunity.

As the shepherdess joined the dancers, the young woman in the green domino drifted off and settled onto a gilt-edged velvet chair on the side of the ballroom.

Emily had barely seated herself when a large figure in a black mask and domino loomed over her. "Well, my clever creature, I see your plan worked," he said. "Your mama is keeping a close eye on your sister and you are free as a bird. Would you care to dance?"

Lord Beddington! It could be none other. She would certainly refuse him this dance. Bad enough she had agreed to trade costumes, but beyond that she would do nothing to assist her stepsister and further her ruin.

But wait! Here was the hand of fate, indeed. Perhaps she could do something to help turn Beddington away from Elyza. Emily allowed him to lead her onto the dance floor.

"You are very quiet for a young lady who has just found her freedom," her partner observed as they took their places in the set.

"Perhaps," she replied boldly, "I am quiet because I am wondering what price I shall be asked to pay for my freedom."

"A scolding, perhaps. Surely nothing more than that," said the black domino reassuringly.

"Perhaps," said Emily. "But it does seem to me, my Lord, that any association with you most often demands a higher price, such as a lady's reputation. And frankly, I am not at all sure you are worth it."

Lord Beddington's mouth dropped open.

At that moment the movements of the dance separated them. As she moved away, Emily's heart began to thud nervously. She rarely spoke with asperity, and frankness, if it caused discomfort to another person. It simply was not her style. Now to speak so to an earl . . . good heavens!

When they came back together, she saw, to her relief, that her partner was smiling. "I never realized you had such fire in you, little diamond," he said.

Now Emily was truly upset. Again, they separated. When they came together once more she said, "I did not say those words to impress you, sir."

"I am well aware of that," answered his lordship. "That is what makes them so very impressive. But we have wasted enough time on words. Come." As if on cue, the music ended, and he drew her away from the throng of revellers.

Emily tried to pull back, reluctant to go anywhere with the infamous Earl of Beddington, but she found herself propelled along anyway. The sound of music and conversation became muted as the earl led her from the ballroom and into a room occupied only by moonlight and shadows. Panic gave Emily's voice an extra sharpness. "I will thank you to let go of my hand, sir. I don't care to be pulled along like a horse on a lead."

"As you wish." Lord Beddington stopped and looked down at Emily, a faint smile playing at the corners of his mouth. "This is a side of you I have not yet seen. I wonder why you show it?"

Emily was beginning to enjoy this dangerous game. "Do you?" she asked archly. "I suppose everyone toad eats you. How very hard that must be, never knowing if there is anything about you people really like. Do you ever wonder, my Lord, if you are befriended merely for what is yours by inheritance—your title and your wealth?"

"You go too far, little diamond," said the earl. "Perhaps it is time to show you one of the things for which I am so well liked." He put an arm around her waist and attempted to draw her to him.

But the beautiful Miss Vane did not behave like a proper young lady in awe of a handsome rakehell. There was no whimpering, no fluttering of hands, no tender sigh. All he received for his trouble was a kick in the shins and the epithet of "beast." The earl swore and jumped back. "I see it is time we returned to the ballroom," he said in icy tones.

"Why, what an excellent idea!" agreed Emily, suddenly all smiles and charm. "I do believe you are, if nothing else, a man of good sense."

Lord Beddington did not seem flattered by this statement. His eyes narrowed behind, his mask and his lips compressed in a thin, angry line. He bowed and motioned for her to proceed him, which she did, wearing a smile of triumph.

This was, indeed, going to be a very entertaining evening, she thought.

Two more dances went by, and each time The Honorable Charles Trevor was too slow to win a dance with Miss Vane. The second dance someone else again cut him off. On his third try, the dainty creature told him she was already spoken for. "But do not give up, blue domino," she said. "Perhaps fortune will smile on you yet, for you look terribly dashing, and I should like to discover who you are. We have met, have we not? Your voice sounds familiar."

"We have met, but, alas, I have as yet had no opportunity to further our acquaintance."

"Perhaps you shall have that opportunity later," replied the shepherdess encouragingly.

Another suitor came to lead her away. The man looked at Charles's bronze, curly locks and said, "Is that you, Trevor, you old dog?"

"Mert!" declared Charles. "I must say, this is cruel of you to steal away the shepherdess when I have been waiting to dance with her these past two dances."

"Perhaps if you look properly forlorn, my partner will lead me back here to dance with you when we are done," suggested the shepherdess.

"That is the least you can do," Charles told his friend.

"Oh, very well," the young man agreed.

The girl smiled at Charles as her partner led her away, and he did a little jig. One more dance and he would have his chance to win the heart of Miss Vane.

But after the dance, his traitorous friend did not lead the stunning Miss Vane back to him. Instead, they headed toward the door. What was this? Was she leaving? Charles hurried across the room in hot pursuit.

Miss Vane was talking to her sister when Charles caught up with her. "Oh, it is my faithful blue domino!" she exclaimed. "I fear I must leave to pin up my flounce, but if you wait for me here, we shall have the next dance when I return."

"I shan't move," Charles declared passionately.

The beauty laughed. "Oh, you may move," she said. "But not from this spot." She turned and glided from the room, her sister following like a shadow.

"There," whispered Elyza as the girls sped down the hallway. "I have reserved a beau for you already."

And I have just effectively gotten rid of one of yours,

thought Emily gleefully. A sudden vision of her stepsister in a rage sobered her. She would take no pleasure in Elyza's ranting when she found out what Emily had done. Ah well, perhaps one day Elyza would thank her.

They entered the room that their hostess had reserved for her female guests to mend torn gowns or repin fallen locks of hair. "We're in luck," said Elyza, looking around the deserted room and untying her bonnet. "Here, give me your headdress. Quickly!"

Costumes were exchanged, and the two sisters regarded themselves in the looking glass. "Remarkable," said Elyza.

No wonder the Earl of Beddington had erred, thought Emily, for the two girls were, indeed, very much the same size and coloring. With Elyza's bonnet and mask covering most of her face, and Elyza's gossamer shawl hiding much of her gown, Emily thought she might even mistake herself for her sister. And Elyza had all but disappeared under Emily's pale green domino and the ornate headdress. Perhaps this would work.

Elyza did not stand long before the mirror. She was anxious to be away. She had skipped down the hall before her more cautious sister was barely out the door, leaving Emily to face her waiting suitor alone. You can do this, she told herself. You are now Elyza. "Oh, dear," she sighed, unconvinced. "I am merely Emily in Elyza's costume." Well, she decided, perhaps I should simply be Emily then. Only I shall be the Emily I am with Papa and my good friends who have known me all my life, not the shy thing I am here in London. Music and laughter floated encouragingly out to her from the ballroom, and with determination she walked back down the hallway.

The blue domino was waiting for her when she returned. She pretended he was her favorite cousin, Edward, and smiled at him.

"I thought you had forgotten me," said the eager young man.

"Oh, no," said Emily. "I am just glad to see you have not forgotten me."

"Who, after seeing you, could forget you?" wondered her besotted admirer.

"You would be surprised," said Emily. "Oh, they are playing a waltz! I am so glad."

Charles took the cue and put a trembling hand to her waist. He smiled down at her adoringly, and she smiled back. Elyza had, indeed, had a wonderful idea!

Chapter Two

The dance ended and the dancers left the floor. Emily looked happily around her, taking in the sparkling candles, the many flowers and potted greens her hostess had imported for the occasion, the gaily costumed people. Out of the corner of her eye, she could see her stepmama sitting by a cornered-looking Lady Runcible and beaming fondly at her. She smiled shyly at Charles and thanked him for the dance. "That was great fun," she said. "You moved us so skillfully across the floor, I felt I was flying."

Heady words for an infatuated young man. "Do sit and visit with me," he begged.

Equally heady words for a young woman who never heard them. "Very well," she agreed. "Flying is rather tiring."

Charles escorted her to a chair and sat down next to her. "I cannot believe my good fortune," he said. "I have not only had the opportunity to waltz with the woman I have been admiring for so long, but I now have her to myself."

"But not for long," cautioned Emily, unfurling her fan. "For I shall most likely want to dance again."

"Then dance with me," urged Charles.

"I can hardly stand up with you for two dances in a row," said Emily primly.

"Oh, but this is a masked ball. When we hide behind a mask, we can do many things we might never have the courage to do otherwise," said Charles.

How true, thought Emily. She would never have felt so comfortable, so free to flirt with a stranger if laboring under the handicap of her plainness.

"Promise me the next dance," Charles begged.

"People would think we were practically engaged," protested Emily laughingly.

"I should like that," he declared. "Perhaps I shall come to your house tomorrow and ask your father for your hand in marriage."

Emily giggled. "And perhaps I shall accept you. But only if you turn out to be a handsome prince."

"Oh, I am a prince of a fellow, I can assure you," said Charles. "All my friends tell me so."

"Then you may call on me," said Emily grandly.

"And I shall ask for your hand," said Charles, just as grandly.

"And how shall you be able to do that when you have not my name?"

"Perhaps I already know it."

"Oh, I think not," said Emily.

"Then I shall guess it," he said. "If you give me a hint."

"I will give you a hint. Let me see." She tapped her chin thoughtfully with her fan and smiled. "I have it," she said. "Here, then, is your hint. If you think me conceited, you may guess my name."

Charles laughed. "Oh, very clever," he said. "Truth to

tell, I already knew your last name. But there are two of you. How will I know for which sister to ask?"

"That is a very good question," laughed Emily. "How will you know?"

Charles smiled. "I shall ask your father for the cleverest," he said.

"My sister is clever, too," replied Emily.

"Then I shall ask him for the prettiest."

"My sister is much prettier than I," said Emily, her voice not quite so gay.

"Then I shall ask for the youngest."

"My sister is . . ."

"Younger," Charles finished with her. "Very well. I shall ask for—"

"The next dance," Emily interrupted him. "The music is starting. Do let us go and dance before someone comes and claims me."

While her sister flirted merrily, the pale green domino glided along the edge of the dance floor, laughingly refusing all introductions and solicitations for the next dance. She boldly made her way to the punch bowl, where a large, dark-haired gentleman in a black domino stood, receiving a cup from a footman. "An excellent idea," she said, pointing to his cup. "It is terribly warm in here."

The black domino lounged against the wall and regarded her. "Do not tell me you have decided to be friendly," he said.

"Why, when have I ever been unfriendly?" she exclaimed.

The black domino said nothing, but continued to watch her. He took a drink of punch.

Elyza began to fidget. "I would have found you sooner, but I have only just now exchanged costumes with my sister," she said nervously.

"You have only now, just these past few minutes—" he began, and she nodded. He stood for a moment, cogitating. Then a slow smile grew on his face, and he shook his head and chuckled.

"What is so funny?" Elyza demanded.

"Never mind, little diamond," said the earl. "Let us go in search of refreshment."

Mrs. Vane, figuring that masked balls were for the young people, had settled for simply draping her plump figure in a rose pink domino. Now she sat on the edge of the dance floor, smiling indulgently as her daughter stood up to dance. "Oh, my," she said presently. "That looks like the very same man with whom Elyza stood up for the last dance. What can she be thinking of?"

"I don't know," said Lady Runcible. "But if I were you, Harriett, I would worry less about Elyza and keep a more careful eye on Emily."

She pointed with her fan, and Mrs. Vane looked just in time to see her eldest daughter disappearing from the ballroom in the company of a tall, dark man in a black mask and domino. "Mercy!" she exclaimed, and jumped from her seat to set off in hot pursuit.

Lady Runcible smiled maliciously and sailed off to enjoy the rest of the evening free of her cousin's unwanted company.

Lord Beddington led Elyza into the conservatory. The moonlight shone through French doors, casting magical squares of light in the darkened room, and Elyza's heart began to race. "You said we should go in search of refreshment," she said. "There is no refreshment here."

"Oh, but there is," he murmured, taking her hand and kissing it. "One taste from those exquisite lips will refresh me considerably." He put an arm around Elyza's waist and drew her gently to him. "Come here, lovely creature," he whispered.

Elyza came, lips parted in breathless anticipation, eyes wide and wondering.

Beddington was a connoisseur of women and an expert in love making. He pressed aside a golden curl and planted a soft kiss at the base of Elyza's neck, then another further up. She moaned softly, and he smiled and whispered that she was beautiful as he brushed her tiny ear with his lips. "You are not afraid, are you, pretty creature?" he murmured.

"Only a little," whispered Elyza.

Beddington pulled her closer yet and pressed his lips to hers.

"Emily!"

The couple sprang apart. "Mama," croaked Elyza.

"We will be going now," said Mrs. Vane sternly. "Come."

Elyza fled. Mrs. Vane glared at the evil man in black, who merely smiled and bowed to her. She turned and followed her daughter from the room, her cheeks burning an angry red. She knew, of course, if she'd had any social power at all, she could have claimed her daughter had been compromised and snared her a husband then and there. Alas, Mrs. Vane lacked the social power to bring this particular gentleman up to scratch—if he was whom she suspected he was.

She left her daughter in the entrance hall in the company of two footmen. "Wait here while I fetch your sister," she commanded. "And do not speak to anyone."

Elyza bit her lip and nodded.

A set of lively country dances had just ended, and Charles and Emily were leaving the floor laughing and gasping for breath. "That was even more fun than before," said Emily.

"Did you feel as if you were flying again?" teased Charles.

"Yes. But I have learned one should be careful when one is flying."

"Yes," Charles agreed. "For you never know who you may fly into."

Emily blushed. "That poor woman. I did not mean to knock her into her partner."

"Quite frankly, I think she enjoyed it," said Charles wickedly, and Emily giggled. Masked balls were such fun!

"Who is this approaching?" asked Charles, indicating the plump woman in the pink domino bearing down on them. "Is it your mama?"

Emily watch her stepmama approach in dismay. Oh, dear. What could be amiss? Mama certainly did look cross. Surely she could not be angry because Emily had danced two dances in a row with the blue domino.

"I am sorry to tear you away when you are having such fun, my love," said Mrs. Vane, "but I am afraid your sister has developed a headache, and we must go home."

Emily's spirits fell. She had been having such a good time.

Charles bowed over her hand. "I have enjoyed the

pleasure of your company, fair shepherdess. I am sure we shall meet again soon." And he smiled, a smile that seemed to be just for her.

"I hope so," said Emily. And as her mama led her away, she turned and smiled at him again over her shoulder.

It was only after they had bid their hostess goodnight and left the ball that she lost her smile. She realized with a sad, sinking feeling that she hadn't learned her merry companion's name. Now she would never know who the blue domino was. How would she ever find him again?

Her evening went from bad to worse when the ladies entered their hired carriage and her stepmama turned to Elyza and said, "Emily! What could you possibly have been thinking of, to wander off alone with that man and let him take such liberties?"

"But Mama, I'm Emily," protested the poor innocent, removing her mask.

Mrs. Vane's eyes widened in astonishment as Elyza, too, removed her mask. She looked from one girl to another. "What is this? What have you girls been up to?" she demanded, now even angrier than she was a moment before. "What tricks have you been playing?"

Elyza began to cry. "It was Emily's idea," she wailed and pointed an accusing finger at her stepsister.

"My idea!" exclaimed Emily. The wicked little traitor! "Mama," Emily began.

Mrs. Vane rounded on her eldest. "Of all the foolish, crack-brained things to do! Have you no sense?"

"But Mama—"

"Say no more," Mrs. Vane interrupted. "I am thoroughly disgusted with you. You have led your sister into all kinds of mischief with your foolish deception. What will come of this heaven only knows. Whatever were you thinking of?" she demanded.

Emily opened her mouth to speak.

"I told you, I wish to hear nothing more from you, young lady," said her stepmama sternly. "I simply cannot imagine what could have possessed you ..."

At last Mrs. Vane ran out of words and sat angrily tapping on her reticule. Her daughters sat in trembling silence, waiting for the next outburst, which came only a moment later. "Oh, it does not bear thinking of!" declared Mrs. Vane. "And that man." She turned to Elyza. "Who is he? Do you know him?"

Elyza stubbornly clamped her lips shut and regarded her mother defiantly.

Mrs. Vane grabbed her daughter's arm and shook her and Elyza began to wail again. "You foolish, foolish child," scolded her mama. "What I witnessed is exactly the kind of behavior which will leave you at the end of the season without one single proposal of marriage. Oh, I am disgusted with you both!"

And so Mrs. Vane continued, even after the carriage stopped in front of the house and the steps were let down. The harangue went on, all the way up the walk and to the door, and stopped only at the sight of the butler.

Finally, tired of talking at her daughters, she set them free by sending them off to bed, and went in search of her husband, to whom she would pour out her woeful tale of their perfidy.

"I thank you kindly." hissed Emily as the girls made their way up the stairs, "for putting me in Mama's black books. Wicked creature."

"Oh, stop, do," Elyza hissed back. "You saw how angry Mama was with me already."

"And whose fault was that?" pointed out Emily.

Elyza ignored this comment. "If she found out it was Beddington whom I was kissing—"

"Beddington!" interrupted Emily. So, she had failed to discourage that horrid man after all! "Oh, whatever is going to come of all this?" she moaned. "He will ruin you yet."

"Stuff," scoffed Elyza. "I have not met the man I cannot handle."

"You have not met that many. A few squire's sons with no more town bronze than a fish, they can hardly count. Your beauty is surely wasted on you, for you are not using it wisely at all."

"Oh, and I suppose if you were me, you would manage much better. Well, you were me, and how did you do? Whom did you captivate tonight?"

"That is my affair," replied Emily mysteriously.

"With your face you will never captivate anyone but a peasant," taunted Elyza.

"I may not be beautiful, but at least I am not a fool," Emily retorted, stung.

"Fool!" Elyza's voice was rising. "We shall see who is a fool and who is not. When Beddington marries me, I shall do nothing to help you find a husband. Nothing!" With that she stalked off to her room and slammed the door and left Emily wondering how she had wound up shouldering the blame for the night's disaster.

Her papa blamed her not at all. "I warned you, Harriett," he said to his wife, "what would come of taking the girls to a masked ball. Such things are little more than an excuse for license."

"Yes, but Lady Selwyn was giving it," protested Mrs. Vane. "And I am sure I saw Lady Jersey, herself, there."

"Lady Jersey's judgement, from what I hear, often

leaves much to be desired," said Mr. Vane, removing his spectacles and polishing them.

Mrs. Vane sighed in irritation. "I declare, Mr. Vane, you have wandered far from the subject."

Mr. Vane pointed out that this should not bother his wife at all as she, herself, did it frequently.

Mrs. Vane was not amused. "What are you going to do about this?" she demanded.

"For the moment, nothing," said her husband. "I strongly suspect that if we were to look deeply into this, we should find Elyza, and not Emily at the bottom of it."

"Emily has always been your favorite," said his wife in disgust. "My poor little Elyza—"

"Has, unfortunately, been very spoilt. And that is, I am afraid, as much my fault as yours," sighed Mr. Vane. "Come, my love. You are refining too much upon this. I am sure Elyza's reputation is still intact, so she is none the worse for her escapade. But you had best watch her more carefully in the future, especially if it was Lord Beddington with whom you saw her. The man does have a reputation."

"I am well aware of that," said his wife. "And I have been at pains to explain to her that she will get no proposal of marriage from the likes of him."

"Explanations are not always enough for Elyza."

"Well, what shall we do?"

"For now? We shall go to bed," said Mr. Vane, rising from his chair, "and see what the morning brings."

The morning brought The Honorable Charles Trevor, determined upon the course he had so rashly set the night before.

Whether or not it was a wise course, he supposed there would be some debate. His mama was bound to say he was too young even to be thinking of marriage. But then, Mama had always been in the habit of thinking him too young. Too young to ride to hounds, too young to go away to school, too young to take up his own quarters in town. Charles shook his head in loving exasperation. Well, this was his second season as a town beau, and he supposed he knew the ropes by now.

Naturally, his family wished him to marry a lady of birth and fortune. But while Miss Vane was not of exalted birth, she was hardly a cit or a scullery maid. Her family must have some position in society, Charles reasoned, else they would hardly be seen at *ton* parties. Well, one could gain entrance to some *ton* parties, he admitted. But Almack's! It was dashed hard to get into Almack's, and he had seen the Vane family there only the week before. As for fortune, he had heard little said about the family's financial prospects, but he was sure her family was not poor. And neither was his, so he guessed he and Miss Vane would rub along quite nicely.

Having settled all possible arguments to his satisfaction, Charles had set off to discover where the Vane family lived. This information he knew he could acquire from his knowing friend, The Honorable Frederick Merriweather.

He had found his friend still dressing, and after spending some time helping Frederick in the difficult decision of which waistcoat to wear, had obtained the information he sought.

"I say, if you are planning to pay a morning call, I shall be glad to accompany you," offered Frederick.

"I am not paying a morning call," said Charles. "I am about to ask for Miss Vane's hand in marriage, and I have reason to believe she will not be loathe to accept me."

Frederick's mouth dropped open. "I say, old man! She is a diamond. But this is dashed hasty. Don't you think you should give a little more consideration before setting your foot in parson's mousetrap?"

"I have considered," said Charles. "And the more I consider, the better I like the idea. Besides, if I wait too long, some other fellow will slip in ahead of me."

"That is a possibility," admitted Frederick. "I must say, I was considering it myself."

"I am afraid you are too late," said Charles proudly. "As I said, the lady, herself, has as good as accepted me."

"Lucky dog," said Frederick. "Well, I am going to toddle over to the club. Come by and let me know how your luck has run."

"I shall," Charles promised.

An hour later he found himself being ushered into Mr. Vane's library. There was nothing intimidating about the portly, bespectacled gentleman with a few wisps of gray hair combed over a shiny pate, but Charles swallowed hard anyway, and tugged at his suddenly tightening cravat.

"Mr. Trevor," said Mr. Vane kindly. "I have not met your father, Lord Fairwood, but I have, naturally, heard of him. It is a pleasure to meet his son."

"Thank you," squeaked Charles.

Mr. Vane smiled and begged him to be seated, offering him sherry.

Charles's mouth felt exceedingly dry, but he refused, anxious to have the interview completed as swiftly as possible. He cleared his throat and began his speech. "I have come, sir, to ask for your daughter's hand in marriage. And I would hope that since you know my father to be a good and honorable man, you would be inclined to trust that I am the same. My family has money and position, and I believe I can offer your daughter a secure and happy future."

Mr. Vane blinked in surprise at this speech, but recovered himself sufficiently to remove his spectacles and polish them. "I have two daughters," he said. "For which one are you asking, Emily or Elyza?"

"For, er, your eldest," said Charles, remembering his conversation the night before.

Mr. Vane blinked again. "Emily?"

"Is she your eldest?" asked Charles.

"Yes," replied Mr. Vane slowly.

"Then that is the one I want," said Charles firmly. Still Mr. Vane seemed to hesitate. "I believe your daughter is not averse to my suit," Charles added.

"Very well," said Mr. Vane suddenly, rising. "I should like to speak with my daughter before giving you my answer. If you would care to wait in the drawing room?"

Charles was duly shown to the drawing room to pace and await the outcome of Mr. Vane's conversation with his daughter.

Emily had just finished dressing when her papa's summons arrived. Her face turned pale, making the dark shadows from her sleepless night stand out. "Oh, dear," she said.

"Now, don't you fret yourself, Miss Emily," said Foster. "If you need me to, I will tell your papa whose idea that foolishness last night was."

Emily shook her head. "No. Papa is an understanding man. I am sure if I explain to him, he won't be too cross." Still, she made her way to the library reluctantly.

Her papa's gentle remonstrances were worse than her stepmama's scolds. She knocked at the library door and was bid enter.

Her father smiled kindly at her. "It would appear you have been busy," he said.

"Oh, Papa. About last night," she began.

"Child," said her father gently. "I have not called you here to talk of last night. I believe I know well enough whose idea that was. This is something quite different. You have just received an offer of marriage."

Emily's eyes widened in disbelief.

"Does this take you by surprise?" asked her father. "The young gentleman led me to believe you would be expecting it. He asked specifically for my eldest daughter."

Emily made a frantic mental search among her few admirers. Which of the undesirables had she unwittingly encouraged?

"If you had rather not marry this young man, my dear, you have but to tell me."

"But Papa, I don't know who has asked to marry me," said Emily.

"Now, that is something I had expected to hear from your sister, but never from you. I had thought you more constant, my dear," teased her father.

"Papa, please don't tease me," begged Emily. "Tell me who has made this offer."

"It is The Honorable Charles Trevor, son of Lord Fairwood," said her father.

"Who?" There was no Charles Trevor among her admirers. Suddenly she remembered the blue domino of the night before. Oh, but that was impossible! What man proposed marriage to a woman he had just met?

"A very pleasant young man," her papa was saying.

"And quite handsome, too. Your stepmama will certainly be pleased."

Handsome! It could be none other than her dashing blue domino.

"If you do not wish to marry him, however, I will send him away," Mr. Vane said, walking to the door.

"Oh, no!" cried Emily.

Her father stopped and looked at her.

She felt a hot blush on her cheeks and lowered her gaze. "I—I wish to marry him, Papa," she said softly.

Her father smiled fondly at her. "Then you may go tell him so. He is waiting in the drawing room."

"Oh, thank you!" cried Emily, and ran to hug her father.

"Don't thank me," he said. "It is your own sweet charm which deserves the credit for this conquest."

Emily ran to the drawing room. With breathless anticipation she opened the door and stepped inside, eyes glowing, a smile on her lips.

At first sight of her, Charles had smiled, too. But his smile faltered and his eyes grew wide. "Miss Vane?" he stuttered in tones of disbelief.

Chapter Three

Emily hesitated, stopped from coming further into the room by the look on her suitor's face. Was this the face of a man in love? This was a man in confusion, a man caught in a stranglehold by disappointment. But this was not a man looking at his beloved.

Breeding won the day. He put on his heartiest smile and held out a beckoning hand to Emily. "Well, my little shepherdess. I'll wager you never thought I would follow through on the threat I made last night. But here I am, come to claim my bride. If you'll have me," he added.

Was he hoping she would say she wouldn't have him? He seemed glad enough to see her now. But she knew she hadn't imagined the look of shock she'd seen on his face only a moment before.

Her father's words came back to her: "He asked specifically for my eldest daughter." Suddenly, Emily saw what had happened, and she sank onto the nearest chair. Well, this was what came of foolish deceptions, she thought miserably. He thought I was Elyza. It is Elyza for whom he meant to offer, not me. But it is me he asked for. The oldest. He is caught, fairly and squarely. She sighed inwardly. I cannot keep him.

Charles watched, half puzzled, half hopeful as Emily's conscience waged mental war with her desire. "What is it?" he asked. "Is my suit so unacceptable?"

Unbidden, tears sprang to her eyes. "Not at all. I am well aware of the great honor you do me. It is very kind of you."

Emily got no further in her speech. The door burst open and Mrs. Vane sailed in. "My dear girl, your papa has just told me the wonderful news!"

Emily averted her face, fearful her stepmama would notice her teary eyes.

But Mrs. Vane was too caught up in the thrill of the moment to notice anything. "Such a sly puss," she said, patting Emily's shoulder. "You never told us about this handsome young man." She beamed on Charles, who was looking rather ill. "Who would have thought our Emily would be the first to become betrothed?" she continued. "Won't Elyza be surprised!" Mrs. Vane turned her smile on her stepdaughter. "Our Emily is a very sweet girl. I know you will be very happy with her, Mr. Trevor."

Charles smiled weakly, and Emily blushed. An awkward silence followed while Mrs. Vane stood smiling benignly on the accidentally betrothed couple and each wrestled with their thoughts.

Charles finally found his voice. "Perhaps you would care to accompany me to Rundell and Bridge," he said to Emily. "I should like to get you something in honor of our engagement, but I am not sure to what your tastes run."

"Oh, anything will be fine," said Emily, not ready to face this new horror.

"Nonsense, child," said Mrs. Vane, still smiling at Charles. "Of course you will want to accompany Mr. Trevor."

"No. I really—" Emily stumbled to a halt and tried again. "Perhaps tomorrow. I am not feeling quite the thing. I am afraid I awoke with a terrible headache this morning, and it seems to be getting worse." That smacked of ingratitude. She tried again. "All this excitement has been too much for me, I suppose," she concluded.

"Tomorrow, then," said Charles gallantly. "Shall I call for you at two?"

"Two would be fine," Emily replied, and tried to look enthusiastic.

Charles bowed over her hand and was gone, Mrs. Vane escorting him from the room and gushing all the way.

Emily remained in her chair, staring into the fireplace. Good heavens, what a coil! And how she would have loved to keep the handsome young man for her very own. Such nice, brown eyes, such a fine leg and fine broad shoulders. And that lovely, strong chin! If only he had wanted her and not Elyza. She felt her eyes filling with fresh tears and decided to escape to her bedroom where she could enjoy her misery in privacy.

But this luxury was to be denied her. She had barely gained her room and found a clean handkerchief when Elyza stormed in. "Is it true?" she demanded.

No sense denying it. Emily blinked back the tears trying so hard to be shed and nodded.

Elyza was looking at her suspiciously. "When did you meet Mr. Trevor?"

Sudden anger replaced disappointment. How dare her wicked little stepsister think she had the right to the heart of every male in London! "And what business is it of yours?" replied Emily haughtily.

"Did you dance with him last night? Is that when he proposed? Did he think you were me?"

Emily was saved from having to answer these embarrassing questions by the entrance of her stepmama. "Emily! Whatever were you thinking of down there?" she scolded. "It was most ungrateful of you to refuse to drive out with poor Mr. Trevor. In fact, I should think any young lady just engaged to such a handsome young man would be more than happy for an opportunity to spend time in his company."

"I really am not feeling too well," Emily began.

"Not feel well? When you have just been proposed to by a future viscount? I can hardly credit such a thing. Why, child, you should be flying."

"She does not feel well because her conscience troubles her," accused Elyza. "That proposal should have been mine."

"What's this?" demanded Mrs. Vane, irritation settling in every line of her face. "What nonsense are you talking, Elyza?"

"He thought Em was me. I am sure of it."

"Nonsense," snapped Mrs. Vane.

Elyza glared at her sister. "He danced with her last night when she was wearing my costume. That marriage proposal should have been mine."

Mrs. Vane dismissed these accusations with a wave of the hand. "Don't be ridiculous," she said. "I thought myself when I first heard the news that there might have been some mistake, but your papa said the young man clearly asked for his eldest daughter, so there can have been none."

Again, she smiled proudly at her blushing stepdaughter. "Such a feather in your cap," she said.

"And, my love," she told Elyza, "if your sister can attach a future viscount, only think what you can accomplish. You should be able to land an earl at the very least, possibly even a duke."

Once more, Mrs. Vane turned a beaming face on her stepdaughter. "Such an accomplishment," she cooed.

Emily rubbed her forehead and sank onto her bed. This had to be the worst day of her life.

At Whites, The Honorable Charles Trevor was voicing the same sentiments to his friend, The Honorable Mr. Merriweather.

"She refused you, then?" asked Frederick.

Charles shook his head miserably. "No. She has accepted me."

"You have secured the hand of the beauty you have been pining for these past few weeks and now you come in here and say this is the worst day of your life?"

"I have proposed and secured the hand of the wrong girl."

Frederick's eyes bugged. "What?" he said.

"I have proposed to Emily," said Charles in the dull voice of a man beyond hope.

"Emily! But that ain't the beauty's name. It is some other curst thing that starts with an 'E'—Edwina. No. Evangeline. No. That wasn't it."

"Elyza," supplied Charles.

"Yes, that is it!"

"Well, that is not the one for whom I asked. And that is not the one I was given."

"But how could you have made such a mistake?"

"I don't know," said Charles, running a hand through his hair. How had it happened? The night before he was dancing with one sister and now, the next day he was betrothed to the other. Was this a nightmare? If he just pinched himself, would he wake up?

"There must be some way to fix this," said Frederick. He fell silent, obviously lost in thought. Charles looked at him hopefully. Surely with all this cogitating Frederick was bound to come up with a scheme. Finally Frederick spoke. "You will have to go back to her father," he said at last. "Tell him all. Man to man."

"And what shall I say? Excuse me, sir, but I have made a slight mistake. Have no doubt that I am really madly in love with your daughter. Which one escaped me for a moment, but now I remember. It is the one for whom I did not offer."

Frederick rubbed his chin. "It does sound a little crack-brained, don't it?" he admitted.

Charles slumped in his chair and breathed a jagged sigh. "My life is ruined," he announced.

"Hey-ho, what long faces we have here," called a cheery voice.

"Hullo Mert, Harn," said Frederick despondently, nodding to the two approaching dandies. "Trevor here has just proposed marriage to the wrong female and been accepted."

"What? What's this?" said The Honorable Mr. Merton.

Frederick related the sad tale of Charles's mistake, and the two young men looked properly sympathetic.

"I say," said yet another young gentleman of their acquaintance. "It looks like a demmed funeral here. What's toward?" On being told, he burst out laughing. "Oh, that is rich, Trevor," he said. "But it is an easy

enough mistake. The sisters are so hard to tell apart."
He burst out laughing afresh at his own wittiness, and
Charles slumped deeper in his chair.

"It ain't so bad, old fellow," said Lord Harn comfortingly. "She seems a good enough sort. And it ain't as if
the girl will control your every waking moment. You
can still have other—" He elbowed the man next to him.
"—interests. Eh? Hopefully," added Lord Harn with
mock sobriety, "you won't get as confused when picking out a mistress as you did picking out a wife."

The others laughed, causing Charles to glower and
bury his chin in his cravat.

Lord Harn clapped Charles on the back. "Just having
some fun, Trevor. But really. There's no reason to be so
glum. If worse comes to worst, you can bury her out in
the country where you don't have to look at her except
during the summer."

"Well said," agreed The Honorable Mr. Merton. "You
shouldn't take this so hard, Trevor. After all, who judges
a man by the looks of the wife he chooses?"

"And this one ain't all that bad to look on," added another man.

The others nodded and made encouraging noises, assuring Charles that things weren't truly as bad as they
seemed. "I'll lay you a pony he gets out of it before the
season is over," said one.

"I'll take that. Bring the wager book over and let's
enter it."

Charles moaned, and his cronies laughed good
naturedly, continuing to assure him that all would be
well.

At a nearby table the Earl of Beddington lounged
with his friend, Lord Averhill. "Here's an interesting de-
velopment, Beddington," said Averhill.

Lord Beddington smiled. "Her betrothed has good reason for looking so down at the mouth. The chit has a veritable adder's tongue."

"Still smarting?" asked his friend with a smile.

"I wonder why I was so foolish as to tell you of that remarkable incident," sighed Beddington.

"Because, dear fellow, you were never so high in the instep that you couldn't laugh at yourself. Anyway, you may now dally with the beauty to your heart's content. It looks as if the sister will be much too busy to throw a rub in your way."

"I wonder," said Beddington thoughtfully.

Meanwhile, the subject of all this lively discussion was at home, hiding in her room with a headache, which had evolved from an excuse for solitude into the real thing.

Why, oh why had her stepmama entered the room when she did? If she had delayed but a moment longer, Emily would have told her confused suitor all and set him free. It would have been hard, but she would have done it. Now, the task delayed seemed to grow larger with each passing minute until Emily was sure she would have preferred one of the labors of Hercules to the horrible interview which lay ahead of her.

Oh, the humiliation of it all! And The Honorable Mr. Trevor was such a nice man—so witty, so warmhearted, such a wonderful dancer.

Emily sighed. They could have been happy. If only she had been beautiful. She turned to her looking glass. Her whole face looked red and swollen. Even her eyes, which were her best feature, looked anything but pretty now. They were red and puffy from the ravages of salty tears. "Peasant," she spat at the unhappy girl staring back at her.

She might look a peasant, but she was a lady of quality, and she would act accordingly. Tomorrow she would set poor Mr. Trevor free.

The next day she was as good as her word. She did allow herself a moment to enjoy the luxury of sitting high atop her fiancé's smart curricle, and she properly admired the handsome matched grays pulling it as well.

The sure way to a man's heart is to appreciate his judgement in all matters concerning horseflesh, and Charles unknowingly forestalled Emily's emancipation proclamation by telling her all about this particular pair.

He finally stopped for breath, and Emily started to make her confession. "Mr. Trevor," she began.

"Don't you think you should call me Charles?" suggested her companion.

"Under the circumstances," said Emily, "no." Charles looked at her in astonishment, and she began again. "Mr. Trevor, I am well aware of the great honor you have done me, and I shall always be grateful."

"Think nothing of it," said Charles, blushing.

"But," Emily continued resolutely, "I think, perhaps there has been a slight mistake." Charles's blush deepened at this comment, and Emily blinked back tears. If there had been any hope left that it was she, Emily, who had captured his heart, his reddened face effectively shattered it. She took a deep breath. "I think, perhaps, you had me confused with another," she said.

"Did I not dance with you the night before last?" asked Charles.

"Yes, but you did not know it was me," said Emily.

"It was you with whom I danced, and it is you for whom I have offered," said Charles, stubbornly chivalrous.

"But it is not me whom you wish to marry," said Emily

gently. "Come, dear sir. Do not let misplaced chivalry ruin your future happiness. I have caused you enough grief already. I should hate to cause you more. My sister and I changed costumes the night of the ball. We thought it a harmless prank. Obviously, it was not. I do apologize, and I hope you will not hold it against me that I said nothing yesterday." Emily hung her head. "I was about to refuse you, but when my stepmama appeared, I found it quite impossible to speak."

Charles was silent for so long Emily finally had to look up. He sat staring straight ahead, at a loss for words. "Mr. Trevor?" she prompted.

"I hardly know what to say," said Charles.

"Say you do not hate me too terribly for putting you in such an awkward position," Emily suggested timidly.

"Oh, no. Not at all. It could happen to anyone. All a bad mix-up." He pushed back his curly-brimmed beaver hat and scratched his head. "But still, I have offered for you. And you seem to be a dashed nice female. Perhaps—"

"Oh, no," Emily interrupted. "We shall stop this thing now before it goes any further."

"Er, well. It has rather gotten out that I am engaged. We can hardly become unengaged the day after I have proposed. Bad *ton*. It would not reflect well on you," he finished, remembering the previous day's betting and cursing himself for a loose-lipped clunch.

Emily sighed and rubbed her head. "Oh dear, whatever shall we do?"

Charles shrugged fatalistically and said, "As we have arrived at our destination, we shall go in and choose something for you."

For a female who had snared herself a young man who was well-heeled as well as titled, Emily was possibly the most unenthusiastic bride-to-be the establishment of Rundell and Bridge had ever seen. She sat listlessly as the clerk tried to tempt her with various pieces of jewelry. Finally, when she asked to see something simpler with smaller stones, the poor man was startled into asking the young lady if she was quite sure.

Charles picked up a simple garnet necklace with matching earrings. "I like this," he said, and Emily, taking his cue, decided she did, too.

Their mission accomplished, Emily was assisted back into Charles's curricle and drove away from the fine jewelry establishment wearing as unhappy a look as she had worn when she entered it. "I shall, of course, return this to you," she said.

Charles looked at her in horror. "Whatever do you take me for?" he demanded.

"I do not wish to take you for anything," she replied. "It was certainly never my intention to fleece you."

"I have caused you equally as much grief by my rash behavior as you claim to have caused me," said Charles humbly. "This is small enough amends."

Emily sighed unhappily. However were they to get out of this coil? Then a thought occurred to her and she turned to Charles. "I have it," she announced brightly. "Let us, for the time being remain engaged."

His face, which had brightened, at her first words, fell at this suggestion, but he recovered himself and nodded agreement. "Very well," he said.

"We shall, however," continued Emily, "not make any formal announcement. We will say it is because we wish our families to meet first. After a short time I shall find we don't suit and that will be the end of it. That way no one need be embarrassed. Well, perhaps it will be a little embarrassing," she admitted, accurately interpreting Charles's cocked eyebrow as a sign of skepticism. "But it will certainly be less embarrassing than admitting we made a mistake in the first place."

Charles nodded. "That is true. But I fear this will not be an easy thing for you. To break an engagement is no simple matter."

"It will be far simpler than trying to make the best of a marriage based on error and misunderstanding. Wouldn't you agree?"

Charles looked at her with respect. "You are a very unusual female," he said.

She blushed and smiled and they drove on, feeling in perfect charity with one another.

It was Charles who spoke next. "I have seen you and your mother and sister walking in the park, but I cannot recall having ever seen you on horseback. Do you ride?"

Emily nodded. "Oh, yes. At home. However, that is a luxury we cannot afford to indulge here in town."

"I should be happy to provide you with a mount. And your sister as well," offered Charles.

"Mr. Trevor," she began.

"Please, call me Charles."

Emily blushed and called him nothing. "Remember, our engagement is merely an act," she reminded him.

"Then we should do all we can to make it as convincing as possible," said Charles, and smiled at her.

"Very well, sir. If it pleases you to offer me such a treat, I must admit I would enjoy it."

"It pleases me," said Charles. "And now it would please me if you would call me by my Christian name."

Emily felt the betraying warmth of a blush flooding her cheeks, and she lowered her eyes and stared at her gloved hands.

"Come now. Let me hear you speak my name," he prompted.

Emily felt tongue tied and foolish. She tried to force her lips to move, but they fought her.

"Is this the same gay creature with whom I danced and laughed only two nights ago?" Charles remonstrated.

"I am afraid not," said Emily. "Perhaps if you were to buy me a mask I could do better."

He chuckled. "That is better already," he said. "I see your sense of humor is returning, fair shepherdess. I think mine must be, too, for this does not suddenly seem such a tragic mistake to me any more. I begin to think I may enjoy pretending to be engaged to you."

These kind words warmed Emily. "Thank you ... Charles," she said.

He smiled. "No. It is I who must thank you ... Emily." Emily blushed and he continued. "Very few females would offer a man his freedom as you have done."

I am offering it, but I wish you did not want it, thought Emily sadly.

They rode the rest of the way home in silence, each busy with their own thoughts, and Charles delivered Emily into her stepmama's keeping.

He was duly invited in for tea, but declined, not wishing to leave his horses standing. Emily suspected he also was not yet ready to face the prize he'd failed to capture.

Unable to secure him for tea, Mrs. Vane invited him to dine with them the following night, which he accepted. He then left, saying all that was proper to his affianced bride and his future mother-in-law.

"Well," said Mrs. Vane after he had gone. "What did your future husband buy for you?"

Emily produced her new jewels and her stepmama examined them with an expert eye. "Simple," she said finally. "But nice. Of course, rubies would have been better. Or diamonds. I hope the young man is not tight with his money. There is nothing more miserable than to have to live with a man who is clutch-fisted."

Emily thought of poor Mr. Trevor's generosity and squirmed uncomfortably.

"I should have held out for a diamond tiara and a necklace and earrings," said a scornful Elyza later. "You told me only two days ago that my beauty was wasted on me, but I tell you, your good fortune is much more wasted on you."

Good fortune? Was that what one called it?

"When Beddington proposes to me, I shall make sure he buys me a proper betrothal present," Elyza continued.

"Beddington will propose marriage to you the day Charles leads me down the aisle," muttered Emily cynically.

"What?" said Elyza sharply.

Emily shook her head. "Nothing," she sighed, and wondered how long she would have to wait before she could put an end to the farce.

Chapter Four

Charles appeared at the Vanes' townhouse at the appointed time for dinner. He made his entrance into the drawing room and gallantly kissed Emily's hand, making her skin tingle delightfully, and she found herself again wishing that she could keep him.

Then his eyes strayed to Elyza, who sat next to her stepsister on the sofa, preening in a pale yellow gown with short, puffed sleeves that showed daintily plump arms, and a bodice cut to reveal just the appropriate amount of soft, creamy bosom. Watching his expression become wistful, Emily knew why she couldn't keep him. How could she bear to go through life watching her husband look so longingly at her stepsister every time his eyes fell on her?

He took Elyza's hand and bowed over it, and it seemed to Emily that he let it go with reluctance. "Good evening, Miss Vane," he said.

"Now that we are to be related perhaps you might wish to call me Elyza," she suggested, smiling up at him from under her lashes.

"Of course," stuttered Charles.

"And how handsome our dear son-in-law to-be looks

this evening," gushed Mrs. Vane. "And don't you and Emily make a fine-looking pair!"

Charles smiled politely, his face turning red, and Emily felt hers blushing to match it. Surely this would be the longest evening of her life. "Would you care to sit down?" she asked him, at a loss for anything else to say.

Elyza moved a little to make room for him on the sofa between them and smiled invitingly up at him.

As Charles sat down, Emily was sure it was not her words which caused him to sit between them, but her sister's unspoken invitation. She sighed inwardly, wishing she had Elyza's skill with men. Alas, such skill came only with confidence, and such confidence only with beauty.

"Unseasonably cold spring we're having," observed Mr. Vane politely.

"Yes, it is, sir," agreed Charles eagerly. "I daresay it is much colder than it was last spring," he added.

"Oh, well," said Mrs. Vane comfortably. "I am sure the weather will soon settle down. I suppose to ensure a fine day for the wedding, we should wait until June," she added.

Charles blanched, and Emily felt an uncomfortable warmth on her cheeks.

Fortunately, at that moment the butler arrived to announce dinner, momentarily distracting Mrs. Vane from the subject of matrimony.

It would have been too much to hope that she would be long distracted from such a pleasant topic, however, and no sooner was the soup served than she again took it up. "Something must, of course, be sent straight away to the *Gazette*," she said.

"No!" chorused Emily and Charles.

Mrs. Vane stared at them as if they'd taken leave of their senses.

"Actually, I have not yet had time to inform my family of my great good fortune," Charles explained. "And I would like to be able to do so before making our engagement public."

Mrs. Vane was all smiles again. "Of course," she said. "Most understandable. Emily and Charles exchanged relieved looks until Mrs. Vane continued. "I imagine you will be telling your family first thing tomorrow."

Again, the accidentally betrothed couple exchanged looks. "My family is at our country estate in Gloucestershire," said Charles.

Mrs. Vane smiled politely. "Then I am sure you will want to set out to see them straightaway," she said.

"Oh, yes," agreed Charles with false heartiness.

"But you must wait until everyone is well, naturally," said Emily, improvising rapidly. Charles looked at her blankly, and she put as much meaning as possible into the look she returned him.

"Oh, yes," he said. "As soon as my sister is over the mumps," he finished triumphantly, and Emily smiled at him as if he were a student who had just remembered his lesson.

"Well, I am sure that has put your family in a bit of a pucker," conceded Mrs. Vane, "but—"

Before she could go on Emily quickly put in, "I imagine you have never had the mumps, have you Charles? And your mother would not wish you to come 'round and risk contracting the sickness from your sister."

"Er, yes," agreed Charles. Mr. Vane was looking at him in a way that made the blood rush to his face. "But

I shall write to my parents immediately," he continued valiantly.

"Oh, no," said Emily. "To receive such news in a letter would be a shock."

"I see nothing shocking about a young man finding a suitable lady to be his bride," said Mrs. Vane, bridling.

"No, of course not," agreed Charles earnestly.

"Well," put in Mr. Vane, "I see no need for rushing things. There is plenty of time to send off an announcement. It is, most likely, better if Mr. Trevor has at least a fortnight to openly pay his addresses to Emily, give people a chance to become accustomed to them as a couple."

Mrs. Vane didn't look happy, but she accepted her husband's suggestion. "I am sure your sister will be recovered from her mumps in a fortnight, Charles," she predicted, making it sound like an ultimatum. "We can all certainly wait that long to make a formal announcement."

Charles released his breath and Emily smiled weakly, and Elyza looked at them with narrowed eyes.

The rest of the meal bumped along, with the guest of honor never seeming quite at ease. Mrs. Vane chattered about their experiences among the Upper Ten Thousand, pretending closeness with at least nine thousand of them. After exhausting that topic, she proceeded to pump Charles for information about his family, and Emily thought she would sink under the table from embarrassment. Poor Charles. He must wonder what sort of family he had allied himself with. Well, it would be a short alliance, so hopefully he could take some small comfort in that.

At last the ladies left the gentlemen to their after dinner port and withdrew to the drawing room. "Such a nice young man," approved Mrs. Vane as soon as they were out of earshot. "And, my dear, I am sure he will make you a handsome allowance. Just think what a wonderful life you will have. You will meet all the best people, go to the most elegant dinners. Ah, how I would have loved to be in your slippers when I was your age."

The future wasn't looking all that wonderful to Emily, but she tried to smile and look happy.

Elyza examined a fingernail and observed that it seemed rather odd Mr. Trevor wasn't in more of a hurry to make his engagement known.

"Nonsense!" snapped Mrs. Vane. "He told us exactly why he wished to wait."

"Perhaps the real reason he wished to wait is because he never wanted to marry Emily in the first place," said Elyza.

"I will hear no more of this," commanded Mrs. Vane. "He has proposed and been accepted, and he will marry Emily just as he promised. And you will say no more on that head, young lady. You will, instead, concentrate on fixing the attentions of someone suitable for yourself and stop flirting with everything in pantaloons. Especially Emily's betrothed."

The gentlemen joined them at this point, leaving Elyza no opportunity to reply. She had just enough time to look insulted before putting on her sweetest face for Charles.

Mr. Vane settled into a wing chair by the fire, saying, "Perhaps my girls might favor us with a song or two."

"Of course, Papa," murmured Emily, and took her place at the pianoforte.

Elyza followed her, standing nearby and resting a hand on her shoulder, the picture of sisterly love. Emily reached for a piece of music, but Elyza said, "Oh, let's not sing that one."

"What would you like to sing, then?" countered Emily.

Elyza gave her a wicked grin. "Greensleeves," she suggested.

"Very well," said Emily calmly. She tried to remain equally calm as she sang the words, "Alas, my love, you do me wrong to cast me off discourteously." Did her sister somehow know that her engagement was a false one, and Charles Trevor would shed her as soon as was politely possible?

Charles applauded them when they were done. "You sing very well together," he said. He rose and strolled across the room to join them.

"Would you care to make a trio?" asked Elyza.

Charles nodded. "Most definitely."

The next half hour was spent singing. The three finally agreed that they had exhausted their voices, and left the pianoforte. Emily found herself thinking how very pleasant it was having Charles around, and what a nice addition he made to their family circle. He is not a permanent addition, she reminded herself sternly, so don't be building castles in the air.

The two men discussed books for some time until Mrs. Vane pronounced herself heartily weary of the subject and began to pump Charles for information on various members of the *ton*.

"Ah, such lovely people we have become acquainted with since coming to London," rhapsodized Mrs. Vane, returning to a subject Emily had hoped she'd already exhausted. "I am sure I have never met anyone so kind as dear Lady Cowper. Such a charming, warm-hearted creature. Many's the cozy little chat we've had."

Emily's eyes widened as the truth, which had already been considerably stretched at dinner, was now pulled even further. So far as she could remember, her stepmama had only spoken to Lady Cowper once, when she'd seen her at Almack's and pressed her cousin, Lady Runcible to introduce her.

"And Mrs. Drummond Burrell," continued Mrs. Vane. "A very impressive woman. Unfortunately, I have been so busy I have been unable to call on her. It is such a busy whirl during the social season, is it not?" Charles nodded agreement and Mrs. Vane continued. "Our only chance to visit was, alas, short."

Emily remembered that, and blushed at the memory. Mrs. Drummond Burrell had put Mama firmly in her place with only a few haughty words.

Emily felt an uncomfortable dampness growing on her forehead and under her arms. Mama was making a cake of herself! Surely she didn't think to fool Charles into believing they were intimate with any of these people? "I wonder where Dodders is with the tea tray?" she said.

Mrs. Vane looked at her stepdaughter in mild irritation. "I am sure when the time comes to bring it, he will be here," she said dauntingly.

Emily fell silent, and tried to ignore her mother's foolish conversation. She caught sight of her father, who smiled at her as if sharing a secret joke, and she tried to smile back. She hoped Charles had a sense of humor.

At last the tea tray appeared and Emily breathed a sigh of relief. Charles could take his cup of tea and his cake and make good his escape.

Which he did in another twenty minutes. But not before informing Emily that he had found a suitable mount for her and one for her sister as well. "Would you ladies care to ride in Hyde Park next week?" he asked.

"Oh, I am sure the girls would love to do that!" exclaimed Mrs. Vane. "Wouldn't you, dears?"

"I should like that very much," admitted Emily.

"Oh, yes," agreed Elyza. "That will be much more pleasant than walking." She sighed. "I wish I had known I would be riding in town. I have only brought the saddest old riding habit with me."

Emily knew which riding habit her sister was speaking of. It was blue, with gold epaulettes on the shoulders. Elyza looked irresistible in it. Suddenly some of the pleasure at the prospect of a ride left Emily.

"I am sure you look lovely in it," said Charles gallantly. He caught sight of Emily's face, cleared his throat and said, "Well. Until Monday. I shall call for you ladies at half past four."

"We will look forward to it," said Elyza.

Emily, who was still sorting out her feelings, merely nodded.

"A delightful young man," pronounced Mrs. Vane after Charles had taken his leave and been showed out.

"He will do very well for you, puss," said Mr. Vane.

"Yes," agreed Elyza casually. "Much better for you than for me. I find him rather dull."

This slur on her quasi-suitor perturbed Emily even more than Elyza's earlier flirting with him. "Well, you found him interesting enough to flirt with this evening. You are just jealous because he proposed to me."

"I certainly am not!" declared Elyza. "When I become engaged it will be to a man who knows for whom he is offering. *I* have no intention of becoming an accidental bride."

"That is quite enough," said Mr. Vane sternly. "I'll

hear no more such unsisterly remarks from you, young lady."

Elyza was the picture of instant contrition. "Yes, Papa," she said meekly.

"Now, let us find our beds," he suggested, heading for the door.

"Yes, Papa," said his daughters, and followed him out, Elyza sticking out her tongue at Emily as they went.

Mrs. Vane started the next week off right by summoning her daughters to her bedroom, where she informed them of her intention to pay a call on dear Lucy. "For I know she is at home on Mondays. Of course, she will want to hear our good news, which I had so hoped to share with her at church yesterday."

"Oh, Mama, must we go?" moaned Elyza. "Lady Runcible is so very stodgy."

Mrs. Vane regarded her daughter in irritation. "Of course you must go. Our cousin moves in the highest circles. One never knows whom one will meet in her drawing room. It can only benefit you socially to be there."

"Mama," said Emily slowly. "Perhaps we shouldn't say anything about my engagement yet. That is, we did promise—"

"Nonsense," interrupted Mrs. Vane. "We only promised not to send an announcement to the *Gazette*. But I certainly see nothing wrong in sharing some good news with another family member."

Elyza made no remark, but her mocking look made Emily uncomfortable. After they had left their mother's presence Elyza said casually, "It is very odd how you are both so anxious to keep this engagement a secret."

"I see nothing odd in it at all," lied Emily. "We simply wish to wait until Charles has had a chance to tell his family."

"Perhaps he is hoping that if no one finds out, he can back out of the bargain," suggested Elyza.

"Why do you say that?" demanded Emily.

Her sister shrugged. "He doesn't give you longing looks. In fact he hardly looks at you at all. He buys you inexpensive jewelry, and you both looked scared to death when Mama talked about sending the announcement to the *Gazette*." Elyza completed this speech with a triumphant look at her sister. "It is as I said. He really wanted me." Her look turned sly. "Perhaps he still does," she added.

"Perhaps you are the most conceited thing God ever put in a muslin gown," retorted her sister hotly.

Elyza merely laughed. " 'Tis true, 'tis true," she chortled. "You tricked Charles into offering for you." Her eyes narrowed. "If you want to keep your suitor, you had best pray that Lord Beddington offers for me. Else I shall have to lower my sights and take Charles when he ends this farce of an engagement." Before Emily could think of a proper set-down, Elyza skipped off to her room.

"Horrid creature," muttered Emily. "I should let her throw herself at Beddington. It would be no worse than she deserves."

But Emily knew she would never do such a thing. Elyza was, after all, her sister, and she had to protect her. Even if it meant losing Charles to her. He is not yours to begin with, Emily told herself firmly. And don't lose sight of that fact or you will be miserable, indeed.

Lady Runcible was underwhelmed by the honor her cousin did in calling on her. She greeted Mrs. Vane with as little warmth as was socially acceptable, introducing her reluctantly to her other visitors.

Mrs. Vane deemed herself on cordial terms with every woman present within a matter of minutes, and so saw no need to hold back her exciting news. "We can barely spare more than a few minutes," she announced. "There is so much to do. Of course, we are all atwitter at our house. The Honorable Charles Trevor has offered for our daughter, Emily." This caused the stir for which she was hoping, and Mrs. Vane beamed as proudly as if the match were of her making. "Such a handsome young man," she enthused. "And so captivated by our little Emily. He rushed right over the morning after Lady Selwyn's masked ball to make his proposal."

"Mama," pleaded Emily.

"Oh, very right, my dear," said Mrs. Vane. She leaned forward conspiratorially. "Of course, I tell you this in the utmost confidence, for we are not saying a word until the announcement is in the *Gazette*."

"And when will that be?" asked Lady Runcible, raising a doubting eyebrow.

"Oh, soon," said Mrs. Vane airily. "We are waiting for Mr. Trevor to share the news with his family. They are, unfortunately, indisposed at this time. Mumps, you know. We don't wish them to be taken by surprise."

"Of course not," agreed Lady Runcible, her voice heavy with sarcasm.

Mrs. Vane set down her tea cup with satisfaction. "Well, my dears," she told her daughters, "I think we may be on our way now. It was so very good to meet you," she said to the two women seated opposite her. "Of course, you must come call upon me. I am at home on Thursdays and would be most delighted to see you." The other two women made no comment, merely inclining their heads, and Mrs. Vane rose and made her exit, her daughters following meekly behind her.

After she had left, Lady Runcible turned to her guests and said, "And what do you make of that?"

Two sets of eyebrows politely rose. "If there are mumps at Fairhaven this is the first I've heard of it," said one woman.

Lady Runcible shook her head. "Pretending illness in the family won't save the poor boy for long." She shuddered. "Odious woman."

The odious woman returned home and announced to her husband that her day had been well spent. "Not only did we see Elyza fitted for a new ball gown, but I have let it out, ever so discreetly, mind you, that Emily is engaged."

Mr. Vane frowned. "I thought there was to be no mention of an engagement at this point."

"There was to be no mention of it in the *Gazette*," his wife corrected him. "That certainly does not mean we cannot speak of it to our relatives and our closest friends."

"And with which of your closest friends did you share your glad tidings today, my dear?" asked Mr. Vane mildly.

"Two most delightful ladies whom I met at my cousin's," said Mrs. Vane. Her husband rolled his eyes, causing the corners of her mouth to turn down. "Mr. Vane," she said firmly. "I don't see why we should not speak of this engagement. The way you are acting one would think we are ashamed of it."

"Not in the least, my dear," said Mr. Vane. "It is only that—" He stopped and shook his head.

"What?" prompted his wife.

"It is only that I am not at all sure our newly engaged couple are happy about their decision to marry."

"What!" exclaimed his wife. "Not happy? Why ever not?"

"That is what I am not sure of," admitted her husband. "But if they wish to take their time in revealing this decision, I feel we should respect their wishes."

"Whoever heard such twaddle," snorted Mrs. Vane. "Respect their wishes, indeed! Who are the young people and who are the parents here? And why ever wouldn't Emily be pleased to be marrying such a nice young man as Charles Trevor? Really, Mr. Vane, how utterly absurd! I am certainly thankful the art of securing proper husbands for their daughters is not left in the hands of fathers. Heaven knows what a muddle they should make of it."

"Well, I don't know about that," said Mr. Vane mildly, "but it would appear the die is already cast so there is now no pulling out of the game."

Mrs. Vane looked at her husband in exasperation. "Why you must speak of gambling when we are speaking of your daughter's happiness I cannot guess."

Her husband chuckled. "Men are a peculiar lot," he informed his wife.

Women were a peculiar lot, thought Charles Trevor, as he made his way to the Vanes' townhouse, his groom following behind with mounts for the ladies. Not only was Miss Emily Vane allowing him to escape the coils of matrimony, but she was assisting him in deceiving her family. He thought back to how she had helped him over the rough spots at dinner only a few days ago. What a remarkably good sport! Clever, too. That idea about him not having had the mumps was positively inspired, and had bought them at least two weeks. Perhaps two weeks would be acceptably long enough for them to find they didn't suit.

The ladies were ready and waiting for him when he arrived at their townhouse. Emily, he noted, looked quite nice in her jaunty red riding suit. She was beaming at him, as though his arrival at her doorstep was a special event. He smiled back. She really was a likeable female.

His gaze moved to her sister and his throat felt suddenly very dry as he beheld the perfect vision in the blue riding habit. Her golden curls were done up and topped with a matching blue hat with a veil. It was altogether smashing, he concluded, as she smiled at him with that delicate little mouth. "Well," he said, trying to sound like a man of the world, accustomed to taking a beautiful woman riding, "Shall we be on our way?"

"Of course," said Emily, and hurried past him. Curse it all! She'd seen how he'd ogled her sister and now her feelings were hurt. Charles felt like a heartless beast. Until Elyza cocked her head and smiled playfully up at him. Well, a man couldn't help how he felt, could he? And Elyza wasn't rushing on ahead of him. She was walking next to him, looking up at him as if he were a treat in Gunther's window that she would like to eat. He grinned at her, feeling like the most dashing man in all of Mayfair.

* * *

Emily tried to pretend she was enjoying herself as they trotted along a bridle path in Hyde Park, tried to look happy, tried to laugh and toss her head like Elyza, but she knew she was making a mess of it. Charles had eyes only for her beautiful stepsister. What was the sense in trying to compete? The entire polite world was out at this fashionable hour of five o'clock, and she nodded at an acquaintance and wished she was home where no one could see her trotting along in Elyza's shadow.

Just as she was thinking things certainly couldn't get any worse, Lord Beddington rode up to them, mounted on a huge black stallion, looking like the devil, himself. He saluted Charles with his riding crop, bowed to the ladies and before Emily knew it, managed to put her and Charles in the lead, with Elyza dawdling along behind them with him.

"Oh, dear," muttered Emily. "I do wish that horrid man would find someone to flirt with other than my sister."

Charles's eyebrows lowered. "Is that rake interested in Elyza?"

"Only in ruining her, I am sure," said Emily. "I vow, every time he is nearby I smell sulphur."

Charles smiled at this. "I can see you hold a high opinion of him."

"No higher than he holds of himself, I am sure," she said. "Oh, do see if you can get her away from him, please."

"With pleasure," said Charles, and his words made a painful little prick at Emily's heart.

Lord Beddington did not seem at all bothered by Charles's maneuverings and cantered up to Emily, who gave him no smile, choosing instead to acknowledge his presence only by a tiny inclination of her head. "You do not appear happy to see me, Miss Vane," he observed.

"Appearances are not always deceiving, my Lord," said Emily sweetly.

"What have I done to make you take me in such dislike?" he asked.

"You have spread your shadow over my sister, sir."

"Is that so bad? I am told I am very eligible."

"I am told you are a rake," said Emily.

"Every rake must settle eventually," pointed out Beddington.

"But not with a girl with neither fortune nor title to recommend her," Emily informed him.

The earl clicked his tongue. "Fie on you, Miss Vane. You condemn me without so much as a trial. I already have both fortune and title. Perhaps I seek your sister's company for some other reason."

"And as I am a lady, I cannot say to you what that reason is," replied Emily hotly. "But as we both already know it, there is no reason to speak it. I bid you good day, sir. I am sure you have other acquaintances dying to speak with you." She turned her horse and joined Charles and Elyza.

Beddington merely smiled at this, bid them adieu and rode off.

"I wonder why he left us so soon," said Elyza.

"He left because he has other people more important than us with whom he wishes to be seen," said her sister dampingly.

"I don't believe it," said Elyza. "More likely, he left because you were rude to him. Really, Em. It is very selfish of you to try and drive away my suitors. Mama will be most displeased with you."

"Not for driving away such a one as that," said Emily firmly.

"I am afraid I must agree with your sister," put in Charles gently.

"And who asked for your opinion?" snapped Elyza, causing Charles's eyes to widen. "We will just see what Mama has to say when we get home and I tell her how you chased off all my admirers," she informed her sister with a glare.

Emily sighed. Her stepmama should be grateful to her for ridding Elyza of a rake like Beddington. But maybe she wouldn't be. After all, Mama did have her heart set on getting an earl, at the very least, for Elyza.

And Beddington was an earl. Perhaps he really meant to offer for Elyza. Even if he didn't offer for her, but managed to have his way with her and compromise her, he'd still have to marry her. Wouldn't he? Perhaps that was what Elyza was hoping would happen, thought Emily with an inward shudder.

But if he compromised Elyza, would he marry her? The earl was a powerful man, well connected in society. With the exception of Lady Runcible, who tried her best to avoid them, the Vanes had no connections. Unless, of course, one counted Charles Trevor, which one could hardly do since he was only a very temporary alliance.

She stole a look at Charles, riding between her sister and herself, and looking very uncomfortable. Poor man. He'd never before been treated to one of Elyza's tantrums. A slow smile grew on Emily's face. Somehow, she wasn't sorry he'd experienced one now.

He seemed relieved to return them to their mama, and no amount of coaxing from Mrs. Vane could get him to step into the drawing room for some refreshment. "I really must be on my way," he said, backing toward the door even as Elyza flounced off up the stairs.

Mrs. Vane followed him. "Well, then, we shall bid you adieu until we see you at Mrs. Drake's musicale tomorrow night."

Charles stopped. "Musicale?" he repeated stupidly.

"Why, yes. I am sure you received an invitation, for it was only last Friday that I mentioned to her our happy association with your family, and the subject of her musicale came up. She told me you had been invited, and very kindly suggested that we might care to attend as well."

Charles gulped. "Yes, naturally. I had forgotten."

Mrs. Vane wagged a playful finger at him. "One must not forget one's social obligations," she teased.

Even if one would very much like to, thought Emily miserably. Poor Charles.

But Charles had recovered himself and was bowing over Mrs. Vane's hand. "I shall look forward greatly to seeing your family, madam," he said.

He took Emily's hand and kissed it. "Until tomorrow night, then," he said.

"Until tomorrow night," she murmured, trying to ignore her body's happy response to the touch of Charles's lips on her hand.

The Vane family's social standing had gone up considerably since the sisters had been seen riding in Hyde Park with The Honorable Charles Trevor, and Mrs. Vane enjoyed the experience of being greeted the following night by her hostess as a social equal. The fact that none of the patronesses of Almack's were present at this particular social gathering bothered Mrs. Vane not at all, for there were still enough people of importance there to satisfy a woman with a foothold low on the ladder of social success.

Emily was happy to see Charles, but she had to admit to him after they had been entertained by any number of eager amateurs that she preferred an evening at the opera.

Charles smiled his agreement. "Even though one must pay for one's entertainment there, one is assured that one will at least receive some," he said.

Emily hastened to assure him that she had certainly received some measure of entertainment from the evening.

He raised an eyebrow. "Oh?"

"I thought it was very entertaining when Mrs. Drake's pug dog began to howl with Mrs. Ainsley as she sang her aria."

Charles grinned broadly. "Ah, now there was entertainment," he agreed, and they laughed.

Elyza, on the other hand, had found the entire evening to be a sad bore, or so she confessed to Lord Beddington, when he found her and led her away from a group of young ladies.

"I know a place where you would find the entertainment much more to your liking," he said.

"And where is that, my Lord?" she asked eagerly.

"Have you been to Vauxhall yet?"

"No," she breathed. "But I have heard it is a most wonderful place, and I should very much like to go."

"Alas," said Beddington, "your mama would never allow me to escort you and your sister there. A shame, too, for there is much I could show you, little diamond."

Elyza looked across the room at Charles and Emily.

"Perhaps Mr. Trevor would take us," she said thoughtfully.

"Perhaps he might," agreed Beddington. "And you never know whom you might meet there." He brought her hand to his lips and kissed it. "Or what adventures you might have." He smiled conspiratorially at her, and she returned his look with one equally sly.

"I am sure I shall be seeing you soon," she murmured.

Chapter Five

Elyza began her campaign to get to Vauxhall Gardens immediately. Leaving Lord Beddington, she joined Charles and Emily. "This evening has been a sad bore, indeed," she announced. "I didn't even have the consolation my sister enjoyed," she told Charles, "of having a handsome man seated next to me." She peeped at him from over her fan and smiled as his face took on a crimson tinge. She then began to fan herself and, sighing disconsolately, said, "I suppose this is the best we can expect from our London season. It is so sad to think some of the loveliest amusements of London we may not see, all for lack of a proper escort."

"And what amusements do you wish to see?" responded Charles quickly.

"I have heard Vauxhall Gardens is a lovely place," said Elyza. "I should so love to visit it before the season ends and we must return home."

"And so you shall," announced Charles grandly. He turned to Emily. "Vauxhall is a fine place. A large pleasure garden with many walks. It has an orchestra, supper boxes, and there are fireworks, and of course, the Grand Cascade."

"The Grand Cascade? What is that?" asked Emily.

"It is a mountain scene, with a waterfall just as you might see in the mountains of Switzerland," said Charles enthusiastically. He shook his head. "There is no describing it, really. You must see it for yourself. And you must allow me to escort you."

Elyza clapped her hands together. "Would you?" she breathed.

"It would be my pleasure," said Charles, and Emily thought how much more pleasure she would take in the evening if her stepsister weren't around to make Charles look at her in that ridiculous manner.

But she smiled and thanked him for his generosity. "We will have to ask Mama," she said.

"Let's go find her right away," said Elyza, tugging on Charles's coat sleeve. "I declare I am so excited! You have positively saved the evening for me, dear Charles."

Dear Charles allowed Elyza to lead him through the crowd and Emily, now feeling anything but pleased about the proposed adventure, followed.

"Mama," said Elyza as soon as their mother was in earshot. "You will never guess what our dear Charles has offered to do."

"I am sure it must be something wonderful to see you so excited," said Mrs. Vane dotingly.

"Oh, it is more than wonderful. He is going to take Emily and me to Vauxhall Gardens."

"Oh, my! How sweet," said Mrs. Vane, beaming.

"Then we may go?" asked Elyza.

"Why, of course," replied her mother. "I am sure Charles will take excellent care of you both."

Elyza turned excitedly to Charles. "Tomorrow night. Let us go tomorrow night."

"But tomorrow night is Wednesday," protested Mrs. Vane. "We were going to Almack's."

"Oh, pooh," said Elyza scornfully. "Almack's is boring, and those stuffy old ladies always look at me as if I were the downstairs maid." She smiled up at Charles. "I would much rather go to Vauxhall with Charles. Wouldn't you, Emily?"

She turned expectantly to her sister.

Emily honestly didn't care where she went, as long as she went with Charles, but she supposed it couldn't hurt to postpone their outing by a day. "Well, naturally—" she began.

"There," interrupted Elyza. "See? Even Emily would rather go to Vauxhall."

"Well, I am sure I have no objection to your doing so," began Mrs. Vane, torn between her desire to show her daughter at Almack's, that shrine of London society, and her worry about offending her future son-in-law.

"Then it is settled," announced Elyza. She hugged her startled mother. "Oh, thank you. I know we will have a splendid time."

With that, she again took Charles in tow, and before he knew what had happened, Elyza and her sister were seated comfortably in a gilt-edged chair and he was fetching punch for them.

"What are you up to?" demanded Emily as soon as he had left them.

Elyza turned wide, blue eyes to her. "Whatever can you mean?" she asked.

"Don't play innocent with me," commanded Emily. "I have been roped into far too many of your schemes not to see one in the making."

"There is no scheme in the making," said Elyza huffily. "I simply wished to see Vauxhall Gardens."

"Just as you simply wished to change costumes at a masked ball," added Emily.

"You should be glad of that," snapped her stepsister. "For it brought you an offer of marriage that you would otherwise not have had."

Emily blushed at this and bit her lip. Charles was returning, and she could say nothing more. But it wouldn't do any good to say anything more, anyway. Elyza was bent on mischief, and nothing her sister could say would change that. I shall just have to watch her carefully, Emily concluded.

Elyza drank her punch then flitted off, leaving a besotted-looking Charles and a frowning Emily as company for each other. "I don't like it," said Emily at last.

Charles shook himself out of his reverie. "I thought it an excellent punch," he said.

"Not the punch," said Emily. "The trip to Vauxhall. My sister is up to mischief, I know it."

Charles frowned. "Up to mischief simply because she wishes to see Vauxhall Gardens?"

Emily sighed. Charles did not know Elyza like she did, and she realized that while her comment might reveal great insight into her sister's character, it also served to make Emily appear spiteful, petty and jealous to someone who did not yet know either of them well. She shrugged. "Perhaps I am just imagining things," she said. "At any rate, it was very kind of you to offer to take us. It sounds like a wonderful place."

"It is," said Charles. "I can guarantee you will have a wonderful time."

I wonder, thought Emily, as she watched her stepsister talking with Lord Beddington.

* * *

Vauxhall Gardens was, indeed, a wonderful place, Emily decided as they made their way along the colonnade. Brightly lit lamps chased away the night. The fragrance of flowers from the gardens mingled with ladies' perfumes and gentlemens' scents and the smells of the unwashed, hard-working bodies of the lower classes to make a heady smell, promising adventure. It seemed all of London was out, thought Emily, as they moved through the throng, making their way to their supper box.

Charles caught the look of wonder on her face. "It is something, is it not?" he said with a grin.

"It is like nothing I could ever imagine," she said.

"And just wait until you see the fireworks, and Madame Saqui walking a tightrope," he enthused.

"Oooh, I can hardly wait," declared Elyza, her eyes bright.

Emily saw how Charles's expression softened as he looked at Elyza, and suddenly the amusement park didn't seem so enchanting.

Charles installed them in a supper box, where Elyza exclaimed over the painting on the wall, and reached to touch one of the depicted maypole dancers. "Have you ever seen anything like it, Em? I think after I am married, I shall make my husband take me here every week." She looked coyly over her shoulder at Charles. "Would you take me every week if you were my husband, Charles?"

Emily's eyes widened in shock even as Charles's face turned red. This was highly improper behavior and Elyza knew it. "Elyza! What will Charles think of you?" Emily scolded.

"I was only teasing," said Elyza. "Charles knows that." She sat down next to the edge of the box and watched the passersby. A young woman of her acquaintance happened by and she leaned forward and called gaily to her.

"You must not mind Elyza," Emily said to Charles in a lowered voice. "Her spirits run high sometimes."

"High?" responded a shocked Charles. "I have seen hot air balloons sailing lower than her spirits."

"She is used to being able to say and do whatever she wants," explained Emily. "It is because she is so very lovely, you see. People think her pertness charming."

Charles's expression softened. "Yes, actually, it is," he agreed, and Emily found herself wishing she hadn't been so quick to excuse her sister's behavior.

Elyza was as impressed with the supper Charles ordered for them as she was with everything else about the evening. There was a dish of thinly sliced ham, the tiniest chickens either sister had ever seen, strawberries and cherries and an assortment of cheesecakes and biscuits, all to be washed down with a quart of arrack. "However do they manage to slice the ham so thin?" wondered Elyza.

"I've heard it said the carver can cover the surface of the entire Gardens with one lone ham," said Charles. He shook his head. "The prices are outrageous."

"But price should not bother you," pointed out Elyza. "You are a rich man."

Again, Charles looked shocked, and Emily found herself blushing at her stepsister's thoughtlessness.

But she had no chance to remonstrate with Elyza, for her attention was captured by the approach of a tall, dark gentleman. "Lord Beddington!" Elyza announced. She smiled up at the earl from under her lashes. "What a surprise," she murmured.

Emily caught the amusement in Beddington's eyes

and her own narrowed. Surprise, indeed! "Are you here with friends, my Lord?" she asked pointedly.

"Actually, I came alone," said the earl.

"Perhaps you would care to join us," offered Elyza boldly. "I am sure Charles would not mind."

The look on Charles's face said he would, indeed, mind, but Beddington accepted the offer with cynical grin and entered the box.

Emily looked sternly at the earl as he lounged in a chair next to Elyza and allowed her to chatter on about all she'd seen. He poured more punch into her cup, as if he were the host of the supper and not Charles.

Emily stole a look at Charles. His lips were pressed together in a thin line.

There was a clanging of a bell, and Charles brightened. "The Cascade is about to start," he announced. "You will excuse us, Lord Beddington?"

The earl smiled and nodded and remained seated.

"But perhaps Lord Beddington would like to see the Grand Cascade also," suggested Elyza.

Beddington grinned at the younger man in what Emily could only think of as a superior grin. "Yes, I think I should like to see the Cascade," he said.

Charles didn't look happy about this, but he politely said nothing, merely ushering his guests out of the box.

It seemed to Emily, as she walked along on Charles's arm, that the crowds had grown. People pushed around them, and she felt like a leaf on a stream, being carried along by the current with no will of her own. She looked over her shoulder to make sure Elyza and Lord Beddington were still behind them. Beddington was bent and whispering something in Elyza's ear. They looked like lovers. "I cannot like this situation," she said to Charles.

"Nor can I," he agreed. "But what can I do? I can hardly order the fellow off when Elyza has invited him to stay."

"I am sure Elyza is up to something," fretted Emily.

"If that rake means mischief I'll cut his heart out," growled Charles.

This should have comforted Emily. It only made her feel worse. Charles would never have been so upset if it were her back there with Lord Beddington.

Misinterpreting her sad look, Charles patted her hand comfortingly. "Don't worry. We won't let any harm come to your sister."

Emily forced herself back to the subject at hand. "Thank you, Charles," she said. "I am sure I am worrying for nothing. What could he possibly do to her in this crowd anyway?" She stole another look over her shoulder and gasped. Lord Beddington and Elyza were no longer behind them. She scanned the crowd and caught sight of Elyza's bonnet bobbing away. "Elyza!" she cried. Releasing Charles's arm, she pushed through the mob after her sister.

Before he quite knew what had happened, Charles found himself alone in the throng. He stood, momentarily dazed, and watched his fiancée charging away through the crowd. Elyza and Beddington had completely disappeared from sight. An unseen hand clamped around his heart and squeezed. One Vane sister was completely lost. And with Beddington, of all people! The other was fast disappearing.

Stop her! As if stuck with a pin, Charles gave a jump and plunged into the sea of people. It was like swimming against the current of a river. Everyone was determined to get to the Grand Cascade as quickly as possible for a good view. Charles was going the opposite direction. He swore under his breath. "Excuse me," he muttered, shouldering his way along. "Pardon me. I do beg your pardon." Emily seemed to be making faster progress than he was, and with each moment she was getting farther away. Charles stuck up his hand like a drowning man. "Emily!" he cried. "Emily, wait!"

Chapter Six

Twice Emily nearly lost Elyza and Lord Beddington, but as they made their way to heaven only knew where, the crowds began to thin, making the escaping couple easier to follow. It seemed to Emily that they had gone a very long way. We must be nearly to the outskirts of the park, she thought nervously. Where is Lord Beddington taking her, anyway? Do they mean to elope?

The two turned down a narrow promenade, and it seemed to Emily that they were immediately swallowed into darkness. This deserted walk did not appeal to her at all, but she bravely followed them. A woman's giggle carried to her on the cooling night air and she shivered nervously. This was the kind of place where a lady's reputation could be quickly shredded.

"Well, good evening, little lamb. Are you lost?" slurred a voice at her elbow.

Emily looked up to see a tall, lanky man with a shock of carroty hair falling over a long leering face. "Most certainly not," she said haughtily, and hurried on.

The rude man fell in step with her. "Say now, what's your hurry? Going to meet a lover?"

Emily's face flamed, but she pressed her lips tightly together and continued walking.

"Won't I do?" persisted the man. He took her arm and brought her to a stop.

"Unhand me, sir," she commanded.

"Unhand me, sir," he mimicked. "Ha, ha! Hustling down the dark walk we are, and pretending we're just out for a stroll. I know what ladies come to the Dark Walk for—"

Before the man could finish imparting his information, he found himself alone, hopping up and down with a smarting shin. He glared at the young nob who rushed by him, calling, "Emily, wait!"

"Better hope you don't catch up with her," he called. "Not if you wish to be able to walk out of here."

Elyza pulled nervously back from Lord Beddington's embrace. "Was that Charles I heard?"

"If it was, he was not looking for you," said Beddington calmly. "I believe it was your sister's name he called."

Elyza frowned. "He wouldn't want Em. He would want me."

"As do all the men who see you," murmured Beddington. "Come here, little diamond. Let me taste your lips again."

"Elyza!"

Elyza jumped and turned to see her angry stepsister bearing down on them. Blushing, she pulled away from the earl. "Emily! How dare you spy on me!"

"Spy on you? I am trying to save you, you foolish thing!" Emily turned blazing eyes on the earl. "Lord Beddington!"

The earl bowed. "I am at your service," he said, the corners of his mouth twitching.

"You most certainly are not!" reprimanded Emily. "How could you bring my sister to such a dark, deserted spot? She may not be high born, but she is a lady. I can only conclude that you, sir, are not a gentleman, in spite of your title." With that she grabbed her sister by the hand and yanked firmly.

"Let go," commanded Elyza hotly, digging in her heels. "I am not a child."

"There you are," panted Charles, running up to them. "Thank God I caught you."

"I am afraid Elyza got lost in the crowd," said Emily calmly. "Lord Beddington found her and was just bringing her back." She looked at the earl, her eyes a challenge.

He returned her look with an odd smile and inclined his head.

Charles looked at the trio of faces and drew his own conclusions. "Very kind of you, Lord Beddington," he said politely. He turned to Elyza and offered her his arm. "If we hurry we may still have a chance to see the Grand Cascade." Elyza tossed her curls and took his arm. He offered the other to Emily. "Will you excuse us, sir?" he asked the earl with cold formality.

"Certainly," said Beddington.

Emily turned her back on the wicked earl. "Do let us hurry," she urged Charles. "I should like to see some of the Cascade."

By the time they got to the site of the Grand Cascade, the show was over. "Never mind," said Emily. "I am sure there is much more to see."

"We could go to the grove and listen to the orchestra," Charles suggested.

"Oh, yes," agreed Emily enthusiastically.

Elyza was silent, and the sour look she wore quickly dampened Emily's enthusiasm. Emily knew her stepsister would certainly do her best to make sure that everyone else's evening would be as thoroughly ruined as hers had been. She tried to make up for Elyza's rudeness by telling Charles how wonderful she thought the amusement park.

Charles's smile was looking a little frayed around the edges. "I wish you could have seen the Grand Cascade," he sighed.

"It is all Emily's fault we missed it," observed Elyza.

"My fault!" cried Emily.

"Of course, your fault. Lord Beddington and I would have found it just fine if you hadn't come haring after us and started such an embarrassing scene."

Charles sprang to Emily's defense. "Miss Vane, I mean Elyza," he stammered. "I think you have no idea of the kindness your sister did you by following you. The Dark Walk has a reputation for ruining gently bred young ladies."

"Oh, pooh," scoffed Elyza. "How can simply strolling down a lane in a pleasure garden ruin someone."

"It just can," said Charles firmly, closing the subject.

Elyza said no more about her escapade, but she had much to say about the rest of the evening. The orchestra was inferior, the crowd was rude, the weather was getting cold.

Charles finally gave up and suggested they return home. No one objected.

In the carriage, Emily tried her hardest to keep up a conversation. But Elyza's pouting silence reigned over the return trip. She sailed off into the house as soon as the steps were let down, leaving Charles and Emily to follow as best they could.

"I am sorry the evening turned out to be such a disappointment," said Charles humbly as they climbed the steps to the front door.

Emily paused at the door and looked at him. A lock of coppery hair had fallen onto his forehead and it was all she could do not to push it back. "Please don't berate yourself. You were a most generous host, and I did so enjoy seeing Vauxhall."

"But your sister," began Charles.

"Is used to getting her own way," Emily finished. "Never fear. It is not you with whom she is angry. It is me. And I am sure Lord Beddington will send her flowers in the morning. Then all will be well."

But all was not well the next morning. Flowers and a note of apology did, indeed, come, but they were not for Elyza. They came for Emily.

Elyza snatched the card away from her stepsister and read, "Sincerest apologies. Beddington." She looked up from the note to glare at Emily. "Why does he apologize to you? I was the one who was wronged."

"Wronged?" echoed Mrs. Vane.

"That is not what you claimed last night," retorted Emily, ignoring her mother.

Mrs. Vane clapped her hands. "Stop this squabbling at once. I will hear what happened."

Two different stories came out, and Mrs. Vane knew which one to believe. She boxed her lovely daughter's ears. "You foolish girl. Did I not warn you about that man? Just see if I allow you to have that new ballgown you wanted now. Maybe if you do without, it will remind you to listen to your mama."

"But mama," wailed Elyza.

Mrs. Vane held up a hand. "Don't even speak to me. Horrid girl. After all I've done to launch you in society, this is the way you repay your poor mother."

Elyza turned on Emily. "This is all your fault! Ever since the masked ball, you have done everything you could to ruin my life. Well, see if I don't do even worse to yours!" Hurling the threat from over her shoulder, Elyza rushed from the room, leaving Emily to deal with the remains of their mother's anger.

But Mrs. Vane's anger was like a summer storm, loud and noisy and quickly gone. By the following evening she was completely recovered and basking in her daughters' social success as she watched them dancing at Mrs. Wattle's ball.

To show his attachment, Charles had come to Emily's side the minute the family entered the ballroom. But she could tell from the way he looked at her stepsister that it was still Elyza who made his heart dance.

Emily tried not to think about it as she executed the steps for the quadrille. Love was truly blind, and no miracle could heal a blind person, she told herself firmly. So she had better enjoy what small pleasures she could and be glad for them. For soon, before the season was over, she would have to set poor Charles free.

They finished their dance, and Charles was just returning her to her stepmama when Lord Beddington intercepted them and asked Emily for a dance.

This will never do, she thought. She looked expectantly at Charles, hoping he would say something to discourage the earl.

Charles frowned.

"Come now, Trevor. Don't be a dog in the manger," said Beddington. "You cannot expect to dance every dance with Miss Vane. Unless, of course, you are engaged. And since I have seen no announcement of such a happy event, I assume she is still free to dance with other admirers." He turned his attention to Emily. "I believe this next dance is a waltz. Allow me to give you the pleasure."

Emily looked anything but pleased, but she let the earl lead her out onto the dance floor, leaving Charles to stand frowning after them.

"Well!" huffed Elyza, who seemed to have materialized next to him from thin air.

Charles gave a start, then brightened. "I say, Elyza. Are you free? Would you care to dance?"

Elyza was still scowling at Lord Beddington's back. "I should say not!" she snapped and marched off.

Charles sighed as the pleasure drained from his evening.

"Why so blue-devilled Trevor?" asked his friend, Frederick Merriweather, coming to stand beside him. "You've only had to dance with Miss Vane once. And, you know, she don't look so bad tonight."

Charles's eyebrows dropped into a scowl as Lord Beddington put a hand on Emily's waist.

Seeing his friend's thunderous expression, Frederick continued. "She seems a nice enough sort."

"She is," said Charles. "Much too nice for that villain Beddington."

"Have you found a way to get out of your arrangement yet?" asked Frederick.

Charles shook his head, still watching the earl and Emily.

Frederick followed his gaze. "Say, there's a thought. Pass her off on Beddington." He clapped his friend on the back. "I've got my blunt riding on you, you know."

Charles looked at him in irritation. "Have you got

pebbles in your brainbox?" he snapped. "Beddington's too old for her."

"Thirty-five ain't that old," said Frederick reasonably. "The man's got a title to boot."

"And a reputation. He's a rake. He wouldn't know what to do with a nice girl like Emily."

Frederick stared at his friend. "What's the matter with you, Trevor? You ain't the girl's father, after all."

"No, I'm her betrothed," stated Charles. "And I'll be hanged if I'll see her thrown to a wolf like Beddington."

"What!" exclaimed Frederick.

"Take a damper," snapped Charles, and left his poor friend to stand gaping after him.

"And he accused *me* of having pebbles in my brainbox," muttered Frederick.

"Usually the only young ladies who answer me in monosyllables are those who are intimidated by me," observed Lord Beddington as he moved Emily across the dance floor.

Emily made no reply, but kept her eyes fixed on something just past the earl's right shoulder.

"I know that is not the case with you, Miss Vane," he continued. "So why won't you converse with me?"

"Because I have nothing to say to you," said Emily.

"Cannot we be friends?"

"I am sure that is what the snake asked Eve when first they met in the garden," Emily replied.

Beddington laughed. "You are a very clever young lady. I admire cleverness in a woman."

"I am not the least bit interested in what you admire, my Lord," said Emily frostily.

"And not the least interested in allowing me to plead my case?" persisted the earl.

"Your crimes are becoming too many to plead," said Emily.

"You should at least give me an opportunity to try and prove to you I am not the arch villain you think me. Come, Miss Vane. Show me that you have a heart."

"I assure you I have a heart, my Lord," said Emily, "and you will just have to take my word for it."

"Of course I should take your word for it, for I know such a scrupulous young lady as yourself would never tell a lie," said the earl.

Emily blushed, thinking of the big lie she was telling by pretending to be engaged to Charles.

"And I am sure you are a fair woman. Which is why you must allow me to defend my character," continued the earl. "It would hardly be fair to judge me on the little you have seen of me."

"I may have seen little of you, sir," replied Emily, "but believe me, I have heard much."

"Hearsay," said the earl. "Gossip. Many a reputation has been ruined by unfounded gossip. No. I am afraid I must insist on an opportunity to plead my case, and this dance will not provide it." He looked thoughtful for a moment. "I have it!" he exclaimed. "You must allow me to take you up in my curricle tomorrow afternoon. Just once 'round the park."

Emily's eyes widened in amazement. "Lord Beddington. I have no wish to be rude, but I can see no sense in doing any such thing. We can have nothing in common. I have neither title nor fortune. I am not inclined to dalliance. And I am not the least bit beautiful."

"Compared to your sister, no," agreed Beddington pleasantly, causing a twinge in Emily's heart.

How sad to hear the same painful truth her looking glass told her from another person, especially a male.

"But you are not wholly unattractive," he continued. "And you possess something infinitely more intriguing than mere beauty."

"And what might that be?" demanded Emily irritably.

"Why, you are interesting," said the earl. "You do not bore. And there are very few young ladies of whom that can be said."

Emily felt herself blushing. "Your Lordship wishes to make light of me."

It was now Lord Beddington's turn to be impatient. "Nonsense! You know very well I am speaking the truth." He smiled down at her. "Humor me, Miss Vane," he coaxed. "I truly do wish the pleasure of your company."

"Well, I don't wish yours!" retorted Emily. The earl's eyes widened and her face turned firey red. "Oh, now look what I've done," she said.

Beddington laughed. "I would say you have just committed a terrible *faux pas*. Now I am afraid the only way you may redeem yourself is to promise to drive out with me tomorrow. I shall call for you at two o'clock."

"Very well," said Emily stiffly.

The music ended and Lord Beddington returned her to her stepmama. "I shall look forward to seeing you tomorrow, Miss Vane," he said, bowing over Emily's hand. He bowed to her gape-mouthed stepmother and left before Mrs. Vane could gather her wits enough to say anything.

Mrs. Vane finally found her wits. "What does that wicked man want?" she demanded.

"He wants to take me driving, Mama," said Emily nervously.

Mrs. Vane smiled at a passing matron and said through clenched teeth, "What can you be thinking of to encourage such a man, especially when you are engaged to another!"

"But I did nothing to encourage him," protested Emily. "That is what is so terrible. I did everything I could to discourage him."

Mrs. Vane clicked her tongue against her teeth. "How dare he force his attentions on my daughters simply because he has title and fortune! I suppose he would like to do something scandalous with you just as he tried with poor Elyza. Well, he shan't get the chance. I shall tell him you have the headache."

But the next day it was Mrs. Vane who had the headache. Having caught a cold, she lay prostrate on her bed and totally forgot her resolution of the night before.

Emily thought of telling the earl, herself, that she had a headache, but she decided it would be better to go driving with him and settle things once and for all.

Elyza came downstairs in time to see her sister pulling on her gloves, the earl waiting patiently next to her. "Lord Beddington! What a pleasant surprise," she cooed.

The earl took her hand and kissed it. "You are looking lovely this morning, Miss Vane. That is a fetching gown."

Elyza looked scornfully at her sprigged muslin morning gown. "This old rag?"

"It must be the lovely woman in it who transforms it."

Elyza preened. "How kind of you to say so," she murmured.

The earl smiled lazily at her. "I do hope you receive visitors today, for it would be a shame for such a pretty gown to go unseen." He turned to Emily. "Shall we go?"

Elyza's eyes narrowed. "Where are you going, dearest?" she asked.

Emily felt her face growing warm. "Only for a short drive with Lord Beddington. I shall be back within the hour."

Elyza's chin lifted haughtily. "I do hope you enjoy yourself," she said. She gave Emily a catty smile. "If Charles calls, I shall tell him you are out with the earl. And do my best to keep him entertained," she added, before strolling off to the drawing room.

"Oh, dear," fretted Emily, as they made their way down the front walk.

"Totally predictable," said the earl. "Quite boring."

"Oh, do stop," commanded Emily. "There is more to life than amusement."

"There is nothing to life but amusement," corrected the earl.

"One would think so to watch London high society," said Emily.

The earl cocked an eyebrow. "I sense a Miss Vane lecture around the conversational corner," he said.

"I am hardly in a position to lecture you, my Lord," said Emily primly.

"One would think so," murmured Beddington, assisting her up into his curricle, and she pressed her lips firmly together, determined not to be goaded into answering him.

Smiling, the earl sat down beside her, took up the reins, and set the horses in motion. Emily turned her face away and sat studying the townhouses in her neighborhood as if they were of tantamount interest.

The earl allowed her to maintain her silence for a full

ten minutes before he spoke. "If I were to swear to you that I no longer have any interest in your sister, could we not bury the dagger and be friends?" he suggested.

"I can see no purpose in it, my Lord," said Emily frankly. "I am a single female. You are a single male. It makes friendship an awkward thing to achieve."

"But not impossible," said Beddington.

"I don't think Mr. Trevor would approve," said Emily, resorting once more to primness, and hoping Charles wouldn't mind her using their temporary engagement as protection.

"Ah, yes," he said. "Trevor."

Emily felt the earl's gaze on her. She blushed and nodded.

"I see," he said slowly. "A very fortunate mistake."

Emily's heart gave a nervous skip. "I beg your pardon?"

The earl smiled kindly at her. "And so you should. Allow me to wish you happiness, Miss Vane. And if I can ever be of any service to you, you have only to ask."

"You can do me one great service," said Emily.

"And what is that?"

"You can swear to me that you will not trifle with my sister's affections."

"As I never had your sister's affections that will be an easy enough promise to make," said Beddington.

"I mean you must promise not to pay attention to her or encourage her in any way."

"I have become bored with that particular chase," said the earl. "You have my word."

"Thank you," said Emily. "Let us shake hands on it. Like gentlemen." She held out her hand.

The earl stopped his horses. He turned to her with a

look that was part amusement, part something unreadable. He took the proferred hand and turned it over, examining it. Then he raised it to his lips, kissing her wrist, his eyes smiling at her look of consternation. He chuckled. "Never fear," he said. "I shall now return you home before you jump to conclusions and think yourself compromised."

When the earl finally helped her down, Emily felt for the first time since she had heard his name that, perhaps, he wasn't so very wicked after all.

The butler informed her that Mr. Trevor was awaiting her in the drawing room. "Oh, dear," she said.

"Miss Elyza has been keeping him entertained," said Dodders, strong disapproval in his voice.

"Oh, dear," said Emily again, and hurried into the drawing room.

She entered to find Charles and Elyza on the sofa looking at a book together. And she noticed that Elyza sat so close to Charles that not so much as a glove could have been inserted between them.

Elyza looked up and gave her sister a wicked grin. "Emily, dear. Did you enjoy your drive with Lord Beddington?"

Charles jumped up from the couch, pulling at his cravat. "Emily," he said.

Emily walked to him with a pretense of calm and gave him her hand. "How kind of you to call."

"I came to see if you would care to go riding this afternoon," Charles stammered. "Elyza was keeping me entertained."

"So I see," said Emily, the picture of sisterly tolerance. She smiled at Charles. "I should very much like to go riding with you," she said.

"Good," said Charles. "I think we should discuss a few things."

"Oh, dear," mourned Elyza, pouting prettily. "Does that mean I shan't be invited to come along?"

"Well, that is, always delighted to be in your company," stammered Charles.

Elyza shot her sister a triumphant look. "Dear Charles, I was only teasing you. I know engaged couples need some time together alone to plan their future. I know if we were engaged, I should want you to myself all the time," she finished, coming to stand close to him.

The red in Charles's face darkened. He cleared his throat nervously. "Very kind of you," he murmured and took a step away. "Well, then, I had best be going," he said. "I shall call for you at half past four," he told Emily, taking her hand and planting a quick kiss on it. "Good-bye."

He almost tripped over a footstool in his haste to exit the room, and Elyza giggled. After he had left, she turned to her sister. "You see? I can take him from you any time I wish," she said and glided from the room.

Emily sighed. So this was to be her punishment for protecting her little sister from ruin at the hands of Lord Beddington. She knew that the just received their reward in heaven. She hoped her reward would be a beauty as great as Elyza's.

During their afternoon ride, Charles broached the subject of Lord Beddington. "I thought you didn't care for Beddington," he said.

"I didn't," admitted Emily. "But I must say that I am beginning to change my mind."

"Well, don't," snapped Charles. "He is a rakehell and a seducer of women."

Emily chuckled. "I think we hardly need to worry about his bothering to seduce me."

"And why the devil shouldn't he wish to seduce you?" demanded Charles. "You are not a bad-looking woman, you know." Emily blushed and he misinterpreted it as embarrassment over his crass language. "I beg your pardon," he said. "My language ain't the best when I am upset."

"It wasn't your language," explained Emily. "It's just that I am unused to such compliments."

"Don't know why you should be," muttered Charles. "There's certainly nothing wrong with the way you look. Beddington obviously likes what he sees. Which brings us back to the subject at hand."

"Yes, Charles, and it is really quite silly," said Emily. "Lord Beddington is a very nice man when one gets to know him."

Charles turned in the saddle and looked sternly at Emily. "To the gentlemen, perhaps, but not to the ladies. He's broken more hearts that anyone can count. And I certainly don't want him dangling after you. The fellow's a curst rum touch."

"Really, Charles," began Emily.

"Emily," said Charles in condescending tones. "I know about these things. And believe me when I say that Beddington is not someone you should be encouraging, especially since you are engaged to me."

"But I am not engaged to you," protested Emily. "Not really."

Charles looked nonplussed for a moment, but he recovered quickly. "Well, not really," he agreed. "But you are supposed to be acting as if you are, and it don't look right for you to go out driving with Beddington. Damn it all, Emily. I won't have it!"

Emily stole a glance at her companion. If she didn't know it was impossible, she'd swear Charles was jealous. She thought for a moment. Lord Beddington had said if he could ever be of service to her, she had only to ask. Perhaps he could do her a very great service.

"Emily, I want you to promise you won't go driving with Beddington again," Charles was saying.

"Very well, Charles," said Emily meekly. "I promise I shan't go driving with him any more." Charles beamed on her, and she smiled back, vowing to talk to Lord Beddington at the first opportunity.

Chapter Seven

Charles made his way back to his lodgings feeling relieved that he had succeeded in warning Emily away from Beddington. Even if the earl's intentions toward her were honest, he would never do for her. In six months time he would tire of her and be chasing after every bit of muslin that walked by and breaking the poor girl's heart. Of course, most women understood about these things, but Charles had a feeling that Emily was more sensitive than most. She would definitely be hurt, and that would never do.

Emily deserved better than the kind of treatment she would receive at Beddington's hands. After all, Emily was a nice girl, a real sport—she'd proved that the day after Charles had proposed. She deserved someone who would appreciate her good qualities. In fact, if he wasn't hopelessly in love with her sister, there was nobody he'd rather be leg-shackled to than Emily, he concluded. She really wasn't bad looking, and she was good company. And even tempered. That, in itself, was remarkable in a female!

He thought back to Elyza's behavior the night they'd gone to Vauxhall and shuddered. Well, she was just high-spirited. All famous beauties were like that, he supposed.

A disloyal thought entered his mind and whispered that living with a high-spirited female could get tiresome quickly, but he promptly dismissed it. He was in love with Elyza, and if he could ever sort this mess out with Emily, he would marry Elyza.

But he would like to find some fellow for Emily who would be good to her. Perhaps Mert? The Honorable Mr. Merton was dismissed promptly. Too flighty. Harn? Harn could be a little stingy at times. That would never do for Emily. Merriweather, then? Good God, no! Well, he would think of someone worthy of Emily. That was the least he could do for her.

But Emily needed no help in picking suitors. At the rout, she watched from across the room as Lord Beddington strolled in well after the other guests had arrived, and wondered how she might be able to attract his attention. She was sure he wouldn't approach her. Not after she'd told him she had no desire to be friends. She watched in the hopes of catching his eye, but he seemed determined not to see her. Well, there was nothing for it but to be direct. She stopped a footman. "Please be so good as to tell Lord Beddington that Miss Vane wishes a word with him."

The footman hurried off to do her bidding and she sat back in her gilt chair and smiled. Until Charles joined her. "Oh, Charles! How are you this evening?"

Charles's brows knit. "I am fine. I wonder you are surprised to see me, Emily. I am sure I told you I was planning on attending this crush."

"Oh, yes. It quite slipped my mind." Her eyes strayed

from Charles, looking for Lord Beddington. She saw him approaching from across the room. "Is it hot in here?" she asked suddenly.

"Well, a little," said Charles. "Would you like some punch?"

"Yes, I believe I would," said Emily. "If you wouldn't mind fetching some for me," she added politely.

"Not at all," he replied gallantly. "I shall be right back."

He set off in search of punch and Emily sighed in relief. She could hardly ask Lord Beddington to help her make Charles jealous with Charles sitting at her side.

The earl presented himself. "Have you decided to be friends after all, Miss Vane?" he asked.

"I suppose we must," said Emily, "since I mean to ask for your help . . ." Here she felt herself blushing. Was she mad to ask a man like Beddington to help her? This certainly wasn't proper. "Oh, dear," she muttered.

"You wish to ask my help, but you fear it is not proper," guessed Beddington, interpreting the message written on her scarlett face.

"I am afraid that is the truth of it," said Emily.

The earl smiled and sat down next to her. "As I said, my dear Miss Vane, what I like most about you is that you do not bore. Tell me what I can do for you."

Desperate times called for desperate measures. Emily took a deep breath and plunged in. "I would like to make Charles jealous," she blurted.

The earl cocked an eyebrow at her. "The engagement is not yet announced and already there is trouble?" he teased.

Emily's face turned an even darker red. "I am afraid the engagement was an accident," she said, watching her tightly clasped gloved hands.

"And you wish the young man to see he has not made a mistake after all," finished Beddington.

Emily still couldn't look at the earl, so great was her mortification. She nodded.

"Naturally, I am honored by your trust," said the earl. "But I must admit it surprises me."

"I should never have said anything," said Emily, already regretting her rash plan. "It was very foolish of me. I know it is hardly proper, but I thought since Charles says you are a rakehell, and he did say I wasn't a bad-looking woman, well, perhaps if he really saw me as desirable, that is . . ." Her voice trailed off and she looked wistfully across the room to where Charles stood by the punch bowl. Elyza was standing next to him and flirting with her fan.

"Yes, I see," said the earl, following Emily's gaze.

Emily forced herself to look at the earl. "You will help me?"

"I shall find it most amusing to assist you," he said with a smile. "The part of suitor to Miss Emily Vane is one which I believe I will relish."

"Oh, thank you," began Emily.

"But," he said, holding up a silencing hand, "I must warn you that I will be giving you my attention for my own selfish reasons."

Emily's face turned white. "Oh, no. Not to make Elyza interested. You promised . . ."

The earl made a face. "Dear child, how many times must I tell you that I have lost interest in your beautiful, bird-witted sister?" He grinned wickedly at Emily. "I find you infinitely more intriguing."

Emily's heart stumbled and her white face once more turned an unbecoming shade of red.

"Come now, Miss Vane," teased Beddington. "There

is no need to look so terrified. I can assure you my intentions toward you are perfectly honorable."

Charles chose this particular moment to return with Emily's punch. Seeing her red face and the earl's grin, his brows lowered. "Here is your punch, Emily. Are you feeling quite all right?"

"I am still rather warm," said Emily truthfully, touching a hand to her flaming face.

"Perhaps you would care to step out onto the balcony for some fresh air," suggested Charles. He turned to Beddington. "You will excuse us?"

"Of course," said the earl.

Charles hurried Emily away. "Why is that man hanging 'round you?" he demanded. "First he takes you driving. Now, here he is, sitting by you and saying things to make you blush. What did he say?"

"Nothing," lied Emily, alarmed at Charles's anger.

Charles whisked her out onto the balcony. "Emily," he said sternly. "I demand to know what he said."

"But Charles," she protested. "What can it matter to you? We are not really engaged, and you are not interested in me."

"I do wish you would stop pointing that out to me," said Charles. "I am merely trying to do the honorable thing and protect you."

Emily laid a timid hand on his arm. "That is very kind of you, really," she said. "But I am sure I don't need protecting. In fact, I have decided I rather like Lord Beddington."

"What!" exclaimed Charles. "Like him? The fellow drags your sister down the Dark Walk against her will—"

"Against her will?" cried Emily. "Why do you say that?"

"Elyza told me," said Charles. He looked at Emily in surprise. "Surely you don't think she would knowingly go to such a deserted place with Beddington."

That was exactly what Emily thought, but she wisely kept her thoughts to herself. What was the sense in telling Charles the truth about her beautiful stepsister? He wouldn't believe her, and it would only serve to make her look small.

The French doors opened and Elyza stepped daintily out onto the balcony. "There you are, dear," she said to Emily. "Mama has been looking for us. Papa is not feeling well and wishes to go home now."

"All right," said Emily, thankful to escape Charles's interrogation.

"May I call on you tomorrow?" he asked.

"Of course you may," said Emily, and noticed that Charles's smile was as much for her stepsister as for herself. She sighed inwardly. What a foolish plan she had concocted. She would never be able to make Charles jealous. Oh, he would feel honor bound to protect her, but his heart plainly beat only for Elyza.

Charles called the following day to find Lord Beddington comfortably ensconced on the sofa, with a Vane sister on either side of him, and Mrs. Vane sitting stiffly disapproving in a nearby chair. Her face lit up when Dodders announced him. "Here is our dear boy," she said. "How nice of you to come see Emily. Emily, dear, look who is here!"

Emily felt her cheeks growing pink. "Hello, Charles," she said.

Charles managed a hello, but it was obvious his mind

was busy digesting the presence of Lord Beddington in the Vane household.

"Hello, Mr. Trevor," said Beddington calmly. "You are looking in fine twig today."

"Lord Beddington," said Charles stiffly. "What a surprise to find you here."

"Not at all," said Beddington. "Miss Vane was feeling the heat so strongly at the rout last night I thought I would come by to see if she was feeling well."

"So kind," said Mrs. Vane. "As the earl can see, she is feeling quite well. Pray, don't let us keep you from your more pressing engagements."

She made to rise, but the earl showed his intention of remaining by crossing one elegantly booted leg over the other. "I have no more pressing engagements, I assure you," he said pleasantly.

"Oh," said Mrs. Vane, sinking back in her chair.

An awkward silence fell and Emily cast about in her mind for something she might say. "Lord Beddington was telling me about Lady Caroline Lamb's book last night," she offered.

Mrs. Vane made a face. "A very unladylike undertaking," she said. "Such goings on," she continued disapprovingly. "And in such highborn families!"

"It is a sad but true fact, Mrs. Vane," said the earl, "that the higher one goes in the society, the greater the mischief one finds."

Emily took in the earl's half cynical-half teasing smile and wondered if he was trying to tell her social-climbing stepmama something.

Mrs. Vane sniffed. "Such disgraceful behavior in a young lady. To behave so over a man. I am sure in my day a young woman would never have done such a thing."

"Things have come to a sad pass madam," agreed the earl. "I am afraid it is because young ladies these days are allowed a great deal too much freedom."

Mrs. Vane raised an eyebrow at the earl. "They most certainly are," she agreed. "And it makes them prey to all manner of unprincipled men."

The reproof amused Beddington. "It does, doesn't it?" he agreed. "A young woman must be most careful of her reputation." He turned his lazy smile on Elyza. "Wouldn't you agree, Miss Vane?"

Elyza's cheeks flushed a delicate pink.

"Of course she would," answered her mama. She glanced pointedly at the ormolu clock on the mantelpiece.

The earl took the hint. "I had best be going," he said. He kissed both the sisters' hands, and bowed over Mrs. Vane's, then made his exit.

"Odious man," she said when the drawing room door had been shut after him. "I would certainly like to discourage him. But how does one discourage an earl?"

"The same way one does any man," said Charles testily. "And one such as that should certainly be discouraged."

"I thought it was rather kind of him to call," said Elyza. "It shows he is not so bad as Mama and Charles think him."

"Oh, yes he is," said Charles in dire accents, and Elyza discreetly changed the subject, talking instead about the ball the family had been invited to that evening.

"Do you attend?" she asked Charles.

"Oh, yes," he said cheerfully. "Will you reserve a dance for me?"

Elyza lowered her eyes. "If you wish it," she said.

"Oh, yes," said Charles fervently. He caught sight of Emily trying to look nonchalant and his face reddened. "I know Emily is going to save me at least two dances," he added gallantly.

"Of course," murmured Emily even as she asked herself, *Why should I bother?*

On the strength of their association with The Honorable Charles Trevor, the future Viscount Fairwood, the Vane family had been issued an invitation to a ball given by one of the *ton's* lesser hostesses. Judging from the crowd that milled about the ballroom, waiting for the orchestra to tune up, Charles knew the woman would have the satisfaction of knowing her ball would be labelled a terrible crush, and, therefore, a success.

Charles knew he should consider the evening a success, for he had managed to obtain the fair Elyza's hand for the first dance. But as he looked across the room to see Emily take the floor with Lord Beddington, he found his pleasure considerably dulled. And as he danced with Elyza, he found it hard to concentrate on her beauty and his good fortune, for out of the corner of his eye, he kept catching glimpses of Emily and Beddington. The dance ended and the two continued to stand talking together.

Elyza turned a concerned face to Charles. "Oh, dear. There is Emily talking with Lord Beddington. I am sure she does not mean to encourage him. But it does appear as if she is, doesn't it?"

Charles frowned. He had been thinking the same thing himself. That curst Beddington! Why the devil was he hanging 'round Emily, anyway? And why was she encouraging him after he, Charles, had warned her against the man?

"Should we go over and rescue her?" suggested Elyza.

"Excellent idea," approved Charles, and escorted her across the room.

"Good evening, Lord Beddington," said Charles. He turned to Emily. "I believe your mama wishes to speak with you," he said, offering her his arm.

Emily had no choice but to go with him. "I wonder what Mama can want," she said.

"Well, actually, she doesn't want anything," admitted Charles. "I just said that to get you away from Beddington."

"Oh." Emily digested this. She glanced across the room at Elyza, flirting with the earl, and wondered whose idea this rescue had been. "Perhaps you had best tell Elyza that Mama wishes to speak with her, too, else she will stand about toadying to the earl all night."

Yes. What had he been thinking of to rescue one lamb and leave the other with the wolf! "Wait here," he commanded as Emily sank onto one of the chairs placed along the wall.

Charles arrived to rescue Elyza in time to hear the earl say, "I have certainly not been neglecting you because you have lost any of your charms."

Charles cleared his throat. "I am afraid your mama wishes to speak with you as well," he informed Elyza.

She frowned at this, and Beddington cocked his head and observed that Mrs. Vane suddenly had much to say to her daughters. "Yes, well, mothers are like that, I believe," said Charles, offering Elyza his arm.

Elyza pouted as Charles led her away. "Does my mama truly wish to speak to me?" she demanded.

"No," admitted Charles. "But it was the only thing I could think of to rescue you."

A frown appeared momentarily on Elyza's lovely face, but she banished it and smiled coyly up at Charles. "Dear Charles. Were you trying to protect me?"

"I was," he said. "Beddington does, after all, have a terrible reputation. And he has already tried once to ruin you. Of course, I cannot blame him for pursuing you. You are the most beautiful woman in London."

These last words were said so wistfully they produced a triumphant smile on Elyza's face. "Do you truly think so?" she asked.

"Of course!" declared Charles. "Any man with eyes in his head could not help but desire you." He suddenly realized what an improper speech this was for an engaged man to be giving. "I mean, that is to say—well, if Beddington wants to pay his addresses to you, he should do so in a proper manner," he finished stuffily.

"Surely it is not improper to speak to a lady at a ball," pointed out Elyza.

"Well, no," admitted Charles. "Oh, dash it all, Elyza. I wish things were different."

Elyza smiled as if at some secret. "Do you, Charles?" she asked softly.

Charles stopped, leaving them suspended at the edge of the ballroom. All the other dancers seemed to him a blur. Elyza's lips were so small and delicate, so soft looking. Unconsciously, he leaned toward her. The high-pitched laugh of a woman somewhere off to his side recalled him to his surroundings. What was he doing! "Well, now," he said briskly. "Let us get you to your sister. She will be wondering what has become of us."

Again, Elyza's lovely face was marred by a frown.

"Emily! Did Emily send you in search of me?" she demanded.

"No. Er, that is—"

Elyza didn't allow him to finish. She tossed her head and dropped her hand from his arm, preceeding him across the room at an angry clip.

He wasn't sure what he had done, but he knew he had, somehow, managed to take a misstep. Charles swore under his breath and wondered if any other man had this much trouble with women.

"You are a selfish witch!" Elyza hissed, taking a seat next to her sister.

Emily looked at her in shock. "What a wicked thing to say!" she declared.

"What I say is no more wicked than the way you are acting," snapped Elyza. "You wish to have both Charles and Lord Beddington. It is wrong of you, Em. You are engaged to Charles. You cannot have Beddington, too."

As if Elyza doesn't have enough admirers, thought Emily angrily. She must covet my two mock ones. "My engagement to Charles has not been officially announced," she reminded her stepsister. "And until it is, I may do as I please."

"We'll see how long you may do as you please," snapped Elyza, and, unfurling her fan, she rose from her chair and strolled off.

Emily watched nervously as her stepsister stopped and attached herself to a group of young women. They took her into their circle and within a matter of minutes were looking in Emily's direction. Charles joined her, bearing two cups of punch. "Now where is Elyza?" he asked, looking around.

"Over there," said Emily, looking at the group of

girls. They were stealing glances at herself and Charles, and she could guess what they were saying.

"Ah, well," said Charles complacently. "At least she is safe from Beddington." The orchestra was starting a Scotch reel. He smiled at Emily. "I believe this is my dance," he said.

There was no sense in telling him what Elyza was up to, Emily decided as Charles led her onto the floor. He wouldn't believe her capable of such tricks.

She tried to smile as they twirled and hopped, but it was difficult. How could she pretend to be happy when she knew her stepsister was busy making mischief on her behalf. A part of her wanted to believe that it would all be for the best if their accidental engagement became public knowledge, and that Charles would accept his fate and marry her. But her more reasonable self knew this was impossible. She couldn't bring herself to take Charles as a miserable captive, and she knew that the more people who were aware of their false engagement, the more embarrassment they would both suffer when they ended it. If only Elyza would not meddle. If only there was enough time for Lord Beddington to make Charles jealous. If only. . . . If only. . . . The words danced in her mind in time to the music. But playing underneath them, in a stronger, undeniable beat, she heard, Hopeless. . . . Hopeless . . .

She hardly noticed when the dance ended, so caught up was she in her thoughts. "That was great fun," Charles was saying.

Emily recalled herself to the present with great effort and forced a smile. "It is always fun to dance with you, Charles," she said. She remembered how much she had enjoyed their first two dances together and felt a stab of pain in her heart.

"Were you enjoying yourself?" asked Charles earnestly.

"Why do you ask?" she hedged.

"You didn't smile as much as you usually do. Are you feeling all right?"

Emily nodded. "Oh, yes," she said, and thought, *Only sick at heart.*

Charles looked at her solicitously. "Shall I fetch us some more punch?"

Surely there was no man on earth more thoughtful than Charles. "That would be nice," she said. "Dancing is thirsty work."

"That it is," he agreed and left her.

He was about to take a cup of punch from a tray proferred by a footman when someone tapped his shoulder. He turned to see his second cousin, Miss Rimple, smiling up at him. "You are terribly naughty, you know," she scolded him.

"Hullo, Mary," he said, giving her a genial smile.

"Oh, no. You cannot put me off with a smile and a hello," she said, tapping him playfully on the chest with her fan. "A fine thing to become engaged and not tell your relatives. Really, Charles! How embarrassing to have to hear such *on-dits* third hand instead of being allowed to be the one to pass them on!"

"Where did you hear I am engaged?" demanded Charles.

"Oh, from Lady Sarah, who heard it from Jane Simpleton, who heard it from your intended's own sister." Miss Rimple looked across the room at Emily sitting patiently, waiting for Charles. "Although," she continued, a teasing smile on her face, "I can see why you wished to keep your engagement a secret, dearest, considering which sister you picked."

Charles frowned. "There is nothing wrong with the girl I picked," he said repressingly.

"Oh, no," said Miss Rimple, not in the least repressed. "She's not horrible to look at. Only plain, poor thing." Miss Rimple shrugged. "I do hope her inheritance was worth the sacrifice."

"She doesn't have an inheritance," Charles nearly shouted.

Miss Rimple's eyes grew wide.

"That is to say, none that I am aware of."

"Then why on earth did you offer for her?" wondered Miss Rimple.

"Because she's a curst nice girl, and she don't waste time at a ball standing around gossiping about other people," Charles snapped. He scooped two cups from the footman's tray and stomped off, sloshing punch as he went.

Miss Rimple stared after him. "How very odd," she muttered.

"I wonder, Harriett, why you let a daughter whom you claim is engaged to young Trevor spend so much time in the company of Lord Beddington," said Lady Runcible to Mrs. Vane. "I saw them dancing together, and from the look on their faces, they seemed to be enjoying each other's company in a manner far beyond that of mere acquaintances."

Mrs. Vane frowned. She looked around to see Charles flirting with an unknown young woman. The young lady was rapping him familiarly on the chest with her fan. "First Emily is seen encouraging that horrid earl and now this," she muttered.

"What did you say, Harriett?" asked Lady Runcible sweetly.

Mrs. Vane looked at her cousin with snapping eyes. "One simply cannot trust young people to manage their own affairs," she said. "I can see it is time to take charge before things completely unravel."

Chapter Eight

Only a few short days later Charles was at his lodgings in Abingdon Street, having his breakfast when he received a morning call from The Honorable Frederick Merriweather. "What the devil are you doing up so early?" called Charles, popping a piece of steak into his mouth. "And why the glum look? Oh, no. Has that rich uncle of yours taken a turn for the better?"

"You've not seen the *Gazette* have you?" replied Frederick.

Charles set down his fork, feeling a sudden loss of appetite. "No," he said warily.

"Thought not," muttered Frederick. He picked up the paper from where it lay next to Charles's plate and began to shuffle through its pages while Charles watched with an impending feeling of doom. "Read this," said Frederick.

"Mr. and Mrs. Arthur Vane are pleased to announce . . ." Charles's voice faded to silence and he dropped the paper.

"Don't know how you think you are going to get out of this now," said Frederick accusingly. "And to think I had my blunt riding on you."

TAKE ADVANTAGE OF THIS SPECIAL OFFER, AVAILABLE *ONLY* TO ZEBRA REGENCY ROMANCE READERS.

You are a reader who enjoys the very special kind of love story that can only be found in Zebra Regency Romances. You adore the fashionable English settings, the sparkling wit, the captivating intrigue, and the heart-stirring romance that are the hallmarks of each Zebra Regency Romance novel.

Now, you can have these delightful novels delivered right to your door each month and never have to worry about missing a new book. Zebra has made arrangements through its Home Subscription Service for you to preview the three latest Zebra Regency Romances as soon as they are published.

3 **FREE** REGENCIES TO GET STARTED!

To get your subscription started, we will send your first 3 books ABSOLUTELY FREE, as our introductory gift to you. NO OBLIGATION. We're sure that you will enjoy these books so much that you will want to read more of the very best romantic fiction published today.

SUBSCRIBERS SAVE EACH MONTH

Zebra Regency Home Subscribers will save money each month as they enjoy their latest Regencies. As a subscriber you will receive the 3 newest titles to preview FREE for ten days. Each shipment will be at least a $11.97 value (publisher's price). But home subscribers will be billed only $9.90 for all three books. You'll save over $2.00 each month. Of course, if you're not satisfied with any book, just return it for full credit.

FREE HOME DELIVERY

Zebra Home Subscribers get free home delivery. There are never any postage, shipping or handling charges. No hidden charges. What's more, there is no minimum number to buy and you can cancel your subscription at any time. No obligation and no questions asked.

TO GET YOUR 3 FREE BOOKS
FILL OUT AND MAIL THE COUPON BELOW

3 FREE BOOKS

Mail to: Zebra Regency Home Subscription Service
120 Brighton Road
P.O. Box 5214
Clifton, New Jersey 07015-5214

YES! Start my Regency Romance Home Subscription and send me my 3 FREE BOOKS as my introductory gift. Then each month, I'll receive the 3 newest Zebra Regency Romances to preview FREE for ten days. I understand that if I'm not satisfied, I may return them and owe nothing. Otherwise, I'll pay the low members' price of just $9.90 for all 3 books and save over $2.00 off the publisher's price (a $11.97 value). There are no shipping, handling or other hidden charges. I may cancel my subscription at any time and there is no minimum number to buy. In any case, the 3 FREE books are mine to keep regardless of what I decide.

NAME _____

ADDRESS _____ APT NO. ____

CITY _____ STATE _____ ZIP _____

TELEPHONE (___) _____

SIGNATURE _____
(if under 18 parent or guardian must sign)

Terms and prices subject to change. Orders subject to acceptance by Zebra Home Subscription Service, Inc.

RG0694

GET
3 FREE
REGENCY
ROMANCE
NOVELS—
A $11.97
VALUE!

"Damn your blunt," growled Charles. "And damn everyone!"

Emily, too, saw the news. Her mother rushed into her room as she was drinking her hot chocolate, carrying the *Gazette* as if it were a trophy. "I daresay no one will mistake Lord Beddington for your suitor after this. I should like to see that wicked man try and bother you now."

"What do you mean?" asked Emily, eyeing the paper nervously.

"Only that now the world will know you are to become Mrs. Charles Trevor," said Mrs. Vane, beaming. She handed over the newspaper. "Only look. Is not that a sight to gladden your eyes?"

Emily took the paper and shut her eyes. "Oh, dear. Oh, Mama, what have you done?"

"Only what should have been done long ago," said Mrs. Vane defensively.

"But we promised Charles—" began Emily.

"That young man has had time enough and more to tell his family of your engagement," said Mrs. Vane, whipping herself up into a fine state of righteous indignation. "If he has not yet told them, perhaps he will now see fit to do so. And high time, I say."

Emily set aside her hot chocolate, her appetite gone.

Charles called on her that very day, suggesting they go for a drive and looking at her meaningfully.

"A wonderful idea," said Mrs. Vane. "There is much to talk about. And much to plan. June will be here before we know it."

Emily looked at Charles in terror. His face had turned pale, but he managed a smile.

"I hope you have found time to write your parents, dear boy," said Mrs. Vane. "I should hate this to come as a surprise to them. But really, with that horrid Lord Beddington making a pest of himself, I saw no other way to protect Emily."

"Of course," said Charles. "It is high time our intention to marry was announced," he added nobly.

Poor man, thought Emily. How tangled in the web of deceit he is becoming. We must find an excuse to quarrel, and soon.

"I am so sorry," she said to Charles as soon as he had joined her atop his curricle.

"Don't worry," he said. "We shall come about."

"But now everyone will know," worried Emily, thinking how hard it would be to give Charles his freedom now that the engagement was public knowledge. All the tittering that would go on over teacups and behind fans. Such a plain thing. Why did she let Mr. Trevor get away? She must be mad as well as plain. Emily bit her lip in an attempt to stem the tears. Oh, it didn't bear thinking of!

Charles had stolen a look at her, and seeing the distress on her face, he said, "Don't worry Emily. It will be fine. As long as my parents are rusticating at Fairhaven, we'll be safe enough," he added, trying to sound like a man in charge of his fate.

Oddly enough, his words did little to cheer Emily, and although he pleaded with her to tell him why she was still so upset, she merely sat tight-lipped and shook her head.

Charles returned home feeling the only bright spot in his life was the fact that his parents didn't know about this bucket of worms.

A short ten days later the note he held in his hand informed him differently.

".... You will come home immediately so we may felicitate you on your upcoming nuptials. Perhaps, you might also deem it proper to tell your parents something of the fortunate young woman to whom you have offered your heart.

Your loving father."

Charles folded the missive and gulped nervously. He suddenly wished he had purchased a commission in the Horse Guards and that he was off somewhere fighting Napoléon's armies. Anything would be better than facing the interview that lay ahead of him.

He called on Emily that very day to tell her of his imminent departure.

"Oh, dear," she worried. "I hope your papa won't be exceedingly angry with you."

"Angry that I have engaged myself to such a kindhearted lady? Come now. I have only to tell him about you, and I am sure he will be pleased as punch."

"But since we aren't really getting married—" began Emily.

"There's no need to tell him that," said Charles. "He won't be pleased if he learns I not only offered for the wrong woman, but mean to cry off from the engagement."

"But it is I who mean to cry off," Emily reminded him.

Charles studied her for a moment. "Emily. If I hadn't made a mistake . . . I mean, if you hadn't discovered I made a mistake, that is—if I were to offer for you, would you accept me?"

Emily looked at him, perplexed. "Why do you ask such a thing?"

Why, indeed? Charles scratched his head, as perplexed as Emily. It was Elyza he adored, Elyza he'd always wanted. "I don't know," he said. "Just curious, I suppose. We seem to suit," he added as an afterthought, and realized that there was a great deal of truth in what he'd just said.

Then Elyza glided into the room, a vision in a sprigged muslin gown, her golden curls tied up with a pink ribbon. She smiled at Charles and he gave her an idiotic grin in return.

The hope fluttering in Emily's chest fell dead. She had thought, perhaps, her scheme to use Lord Beddington to make Charles jealous had succeeded. Evidently not.

"Dear Charles," cooed Elyza. "How nice to see you." Charles's admiring look had not gone unnoticed and she flashed her sister a gloating look. "What brings you here today?"

"I just came to tell Emily I'm on my way to Gloucestershire to see my family."

"So they have seen the papers," guessed Elyza. "Poor Charles," she said softly. Her sister blushed and Charles looked uncomfortable. "Never mind," she said. "Things do have a way of working out. Don't they, Em?" The look she gave Emily was one Charles couldn't understand.

"Yes, they do," said Emily, and the look she returned to Elyza was one Charles did, indeed, understand. It was one of challenge. Emily turned her attention back to him, and now her face wore the same sweet expression he was used to seeing. "I hope you have a safe journey," she said. "And I hope the interview with your parents isn't too awful."

Charles patted her hand and tried to look confident. "Don't worry. All will go well," he assured her and took his leave.

"Poor Charles," mused Elyza. "How ever will he be able to justify offering for you to his parents? When they finally meet you, they will surely wonder what he saw in you."

"Sour grapes," countered Emily, and strolled from the room, pretending her sister's bitter words hadn't hurt.

She met Lord Beddington at a rout that night and he congratulated her on the official announcement of her engagement. "It would appear your scheme worked," he observed.

Emily gave him a weak smile and shook her head. "I am afraid not. And now it is too late."

"Too late?"

How happy she would have been if Charles had come to love her. Then, seeing their betrothal announced in the *Gazette* would have been so thrilling! "The announcement is made, you see," she said.

"So it is," agreed the earl. "That should make you happy."

Emily sighed. "How can a woman who has secured a man by trickery be happy?"

Lord Beddington should have asked her what she meant. He should have given her sympathy. Instead, he laughed. People turned to stare and Emily felt her face growing warm. "For the answer to that you may ask half the women in this room," he said. "Come now, be happy. You have the man you wish."

"But he does not want me," blurted Emily.

"More the fool he," said Beddington. He then kissed Emily's hand and left her to ponder his words.

She was not left to ponder long before her stepsister

joined her. "What, pray, did you say to so amuse Beddington?" asked Elyza.

"Nothing of any interest to you," replied Emily dampingly.

"You cannot have Beddington," said Elyza, "because you are engaged to Charles. And if you don't stop distracting him by making sheep's eyes at him, I shall take Charles away from you. And don't think I cannot," she added.

"I know full well you can," said Emily stiffly. "But I wish you would stop blaming me because Beddington pays attention to me. I am not holding a pistol to his head to make him do so."

"Well, you must be doing something," said Elyza. "Why else would he prefer to spend time in your company when he could be enjoying mine?"

Emily remembered the earl's words and smiled wickedly at her sister. "Perhaps he finds you boring."

Elyza stared at Emily, clearly unable to comprehend such a remote possibility. "That is the silliest thing I ever heard," she said. Her eyes narrowed. "I mean it, Em. Quit toying with Beddington, for I mean to have him."

"Well you can mean all you wish, but he is not interested in you," said Emily calmly.

"How do you know?" demanded Elyza.

"Because he told me," said Emily airily, and left her sister before she could reply.

She wished she could as easily leave behind the misery brought on by Elyza's threats.

That night, Charles was busy with his own miserable thoughts as he sat in a Berkshire inn. He frowned at a fine leg of mutton and poked at a small, red potato, and wondered how best to begin the dreaded conversation with his father. "Father, you will never believe the wonderful woman I met in London," he tried.

He could almost hear his father saying, "If she was so wonderful, why did you not write to us about her immediately? Why did we hear the news from the *Gazette*, via the mail coach from London." Charles could hear his father's voice escalating even as he spoke. Lord Fairwood was normally a patient man, but when his sleeping temper was aroused it was a terrible thing.

Charles sighed. There was the rub. If his intended was such a fine female, why had he not told his family about her? *I didn't wish to bother you and mother when I knew you were both so busy redecorating Fairhaven.* That was lame. What other possible excuse could he have?

He cleared his throat. "I knew," he began experimentally, "that you would not approve of my marrying someone with no title or fortune. But I also knew that once you met Emily you couldn't help but fall in love with her. As I did!" he finished triumphantly and slapped his thigh. Yes, that would work.

And, actually, he was sure his family would like Emily once they became acquainted with her. She was a good sort. And she wasn't so very hard on the eyes. Not really. She didn't have a squint or a moustache. Her figure was pleasing. And she had a nice smile. And a sense of humor. Charles smiled, remembering how lively she had been when he first met her, and what good company she'd been ever since. Yes, he could breathe easy. His family would approve of Emily.

Charles frowned. Maybe they would approve of her

too much. What would they say when he and Miss Emily Vane went their separate ways?

And what would they say if he, instead, married her sister? A vision of the beautiful Elyza came to mind, and Charles sighed again and cursed whatever fool had thought up such a nightmarish event as a masked ball.

Fairhaven was the sort of crumbling old manor house that challenges its mistress from the moment she moves into it until the day she dies. Lady Fairwood was always one to rise to a challenge. When she first became lady of the house, she tackled her bedroom, drawing room, and the nurseries. Then she took on the gardens.

She had gotten sidetracked for a few years with the running of the nurseries, finding suitable governesses and tutors, as well as seeing to it that several important charities remained important and did their work properly.

But with the new year came a new resolution: to make Fairhaven a proper country seat for a wealthy viscount, a showplace worthy of her esteemed husband. The entire house would be redecorated and there was not a moment to lose. For this cause, her ladyship had sacrificed the pleasures of the London social season, and stayed at home, transforming her domicile, room by room, into something spectacular.

Her son had his first glimpse of the fruits of her labors when he entered the drawing room. The butler had tried to prepare him, but in spite of that good man's warning, Charles remained unprepared for the sight of so much red. He blinked several times, trying to accustom himself to the dizzying effect of the swirling white dragons writhing all around a carmine red wall—a wall that had been a restful shade of blue when last he'd seen it. Obviously, his mother had decided that what was good for the Prince Regent and his Royal Pavilion at Brighton was equally good for Lord Fairwood.

"Oh, Charles," cried Lady Fairwood in tragic tones, springing from a bamboo chair to greet her son. "What *have* you done?"

Charles would have liked to ask the same thing of his mother. "This is . . . new," he managed, looking around him.

Temporarily distracted, the viscountess smiled. "Yes. It is quite charming, is it not?"

"How can anyone sit in this room after dinner and not feel like casting up his accounts?" wondered Charles.

Lady Fairwood frowned. "Charles," she said sternly.

"Sorry," said her son. "It takes some getting used to. It is a bit, um . . ." Charles scratched his head, at a loss for words. "It is all the crack, ain't it?" he managed at last.

"Of course," said his mother. "It is the first stare of elegance. And wait until you see the rest of the house."

Charles was spared from a tour by the return of the butler. "Lord Fairwood wishes to see his son in the library," he intoned.

"Oh, yes, I quite forgot," said his mother. She looked sadly at her son. "You have quite disappointed us, Charles, and I know your father will have much to say to you. I only hope you can provide some reasonable explanation for such an odd start." She shook her head. "It is a terrible thing to do to your parents. It has quite broken my heart, you know. I had always hoped you and little Betty Bromwell would make a match of it. I do so like her mama, and with their lands bordering ours, well, I know your father had hopes of his own."

Just the thought of Betty Bromwell was enough to make Charles frown. *Little* Betty made two of him, and no matter how much land they had, it wasn't worth marrying the Bromwell chit for.

"Perhaps your father can help you find a way out of this coil," finished his mother. And on that cheerful note she left her son to face the wrath of his father.

Charles entered the library with a thudding heart. This room, he noted, remained untouched by the ravages of Lady Fairwood's redecorating, and Charles found its manly clutter somehow comforting.

His father's stern face quickly robbed him of his comfort. "My congratulations on your upcoming marriage," said Lord Fairwood, his voice heavy with sarcasm. He took a decanter from a side table and poured two glasses of port, handing one to his son, saying, "I am sure you had your reasons for offering to a girl from an unknown family. Perhaps she is an heiress?"

Charles took a hasty gulp of the wine. "The family is not poor," he hedged.

The viscount nodded. "Ah. So she is a lady of moderate means. And her father is?"

"Very nice," responded Charles.

Lord Fairwood raised a rebuking eyebrow.

"Gentry, I suppose," mumbled Charles. "I met her at a ball."

"So," continued Lord Fairwood, seating himself. "This young woman is at least of gentle birth. But she has no fortune. What does she possess that you were so smitten by her you must offer for her without so much as dropping a line to inform your family of your happy intentions? She must be a diamond of the first water to so occupy your every waking moment that you still could not find time to inform us of your engagement before the announcement was sent to the *Gazette*."

The viscount's voice was rising like a river in springtime, and Charles found his heartbeat picking up speed. He opened his mouth to speak, found he couldn't, and shut it.

"Well?" demanded his father.

All Charles's well-prepared excuses fell away. He gulped down the last of his wine and began to pace. "It was a curst stupid thing to do. I made a mistake."

"A mistake!" repeated the viscount, looking at his son as if he had gone mad.

Charles raked a hand through his hair. "I meant to offer for her sister."

The viscount closed his eyes, as if suffering extreme pain. "Do go on," he said.

"I was in love with her sister," said Charles earnestly. "Oh, Father, you have never seen beauty until you have beheld Emily, I mean Elyza. There, damn it all! You see how easy it is to make a mistake. Their names are so curst alike."

"That would explain it," murmured Lord Fairwood.

"Exactly," agreed Charles. "And when I danced with Emily at that masked ball I thought I was dancing with Elyza. She was so entertaining, so lively. It was as if she were made for me. And she was so beautiful. That is, I thought she was beautiful because I thought she was Elyza. At any rate, I realized I must offer for her right away, else someone else would before me. There were several other men in love with her, too."

"Naturally," said Lord Fairwood, completely at sea.

"So I went to her house," Charles continued, "and

asked for her hand in marriage. I thought I was asking for Elyza, but it was really Emily. You see, I asked for the eldest, and she accepted me." Charles finished his speech and sank into a wing-backed chair.

"I see," said his father slowly.

"Do you?" asked Charles eagerly. "Of course, I was honor bound to maintain my offer of marriage. I could hardly tell the poor girl, 'You ain't the one,' once I had offered for her."

"And she didn't realize you had made a mistake?"

Charles blushed at this and his eyes fell before his father's gaze. "She did," he said softly. "She has agreed to release me. After a time, we shall find we don't suit."

"I see," said Lord Fairwood, taking on a thoughtful look. "And does that seem honorable to you?"

Charles squirmed. "I offered to do the honorable thing," he said at last.

"That is not what I asked you," said his father.

Now Charles heartily wished he had stuck with his original story. His father didn't always understand how things were done these days. "I can hardly force myself on her," he protested.

"Of course not," agreed Lord Fairwood. "And what of the sister?" he asked.

"She is the most beautiful woman ever born," said Charles, and then realized he had betrayed himself yet again.

Lord Fairwood looked at his son sternly. "And so you would throw the plainer sister over for the beauty?"

"I wouldn't be throwing her over!" protested Charles. "I didn't want her in the first place."

"You offered for her," said his father.

"She won't have me," said Charles, and remembering how many times Emily had reminded him that they weren't truly engaged, and how fond she seemed to be of that rake Beddington's attentions, he felt a twinge of bitterness.

"Won't have you?" echoed his father. "Why not? You will have a title. Your fortune is large enough."

"Don't matter," said Charles. "It was a mistake, and she don't want me that way."

Lord Fairwood was thoughtful a moment. "I must meet this paragon," he said. "Your mother will write a note inviting the family to come stay with us at Fairhaven."

Charles blanched. "The entire family?"

"Is there something wrong with her family?" asked the viscount.

"Er, no," said Charles, wondering how he could prepare his father for the toadying Mrs. Vane.

"Good. Then it is settled. The young lady and her family will come to visit us, and we shall see what we can do to put back together your torn honor. For I must say, I consider this entire sorry tale a great embarrassment."

Charles sighed. This had not been a successful interview. And he didn't hold out much success for Emily's plan to end their engagement. She may not have been the wisest choice for a bride, but after having heard the whole sorry tale, he was sure his father would force him to stick to the course he had mistakenly set. His betrothed could concoct all sorts of plans to end their engagement, but it looked to him that the only way it would end was in marriage.

Lord Fairwood had been watching his son. "Don't

fret, boy," he said. "Things aren't so bad as they seem. Your mother wasn't my first choice, either."

Charles looked at his father in amazement. He would never have guessed such a thing, for his parents had always seemed perfectly happy in their marriage. "But you seem so well suited," he blurted.

"Exactly," said Lord Fairwood. "Sometimes fate makes better decisions for us than we can ourselves."

Charles looked glum.

"Buck up, lad," said Lord Trevor, coming to lay a hand on his son's shoulder. "All will come about right if you do the honorable thing."

Charles sighed and nodded.

"Well," said the viscount heartily, bringing the interview to a close. "I suppose your mother is waiting to take you on a tour."

Charles nodded. "I hope she ain't done up the whole house in Oriental," he said.

Lord Fairwood looked pained. "That drawing room makes me bilious. The dining room is Egyptian. Her bedroom and sitting room are full of French froufrou. God knows where it will all end."

"At least she has left the library untouched," observed Charles.

"And it will remain so," said the viscount firmly, as he preceded his son out of the room.

Charles didn't know which was worse, his father's anger or his mother's tour of the house, peppered with mournful statements of how very unfortunate the situation was. And who was this girl, anyway? If Charles couldn't tell his mama and papa about her, she must be terrible, indeed. Oh, dear. What would Christmas be like?

"Mother, believe me," said Charles earnestly. "Emily is a very nice sort. I know you will like her."

"I do hope so," said Lady Fairwood with a sigh. "I had so wished you would marry someone who would be a help to your sister when it is time for her to make her come-out. Ah, well. We are not without connections, so I am sure we will all manage that just fine. But I did always want you to marry a young woman who would enjoy being with our family."

"I am sure she will," said Charles, counting the rooms left to see before he could make his escape.

"Well, if you say so," said his mother doubtfully.

"Really, Mother. I assure you. She is just the kind of woman you always wanted for me." Whatever kind that was, he was sure Emily would fit the bill.

Charles's sister was almost as disappointed as his parents. She had hoped Charles would marry a beautiful lady, who could help her choose gowns and guide her over the rough spots of making her debut in society. Charles assured Gwendolyn that Emily had excellent taste in gowns. But when she asked him if Emily was beautiful and he stumbled over his answer, she looked disappointed and said she supposed it didn't matter, anyway.

Charles's little brother, Phillip, was the only one who seemed pleased with Charles's choice. When Charles said he was sure Emily liked to play spillikins, Phillip gave a great whoop. "When are you going to marry her? When will she come here? Does she play hide-and-seek, too?"

Charles rumpled his little brother's hair. "I am not going to marry her right off," he said. "But you will be meeting her soon, for she and her family are coming to Fairhaven to visit."

Phillip let out another cry of joy and went bounding off to the stable to share his good news with Jem, the groom.

"I am glad someone is happy about this," muttered Charles.

Mrs. Vane, when Charles returned to London with the invitation, was nearly as excited about the proposed visit as little Phillip had been. In fact, Charles half expected her to let out a whoop when he gave her his mother's invitation.

"It will be such a pleasure to go and meet your family, dear boy," she said, and Charles wished there was some way he could get her to stop calling him that. "They are all recovered from the mumps?" she asked.

"Beg pardon?" said Charles.

"The mumps," repeated Mrs. Vane.

"You remember, Charles," prompted Emily. "The mumps. That was why we waited to tell your family of our engagement."

"Oh, yes," said Charles, his face pink. "Yes, they are quite recovered," he said.

"This will be most delightful." Mrs. Vane showed the note to her daughter. "See here? They ask us to stay for as long as we wish. How very gracious. Of course, we shan't stay beyond six weeks."

Six weeks? Charles gulped.

"Mr. Vane will be so thrilled when he comes home and hears this news."

Charles was still mulling over Mrs. Vane's last words. Six weeks. Surely his parents hadn't thought to have the Vanes with them that long. A fortnight, or perhaps three weeks. But six? Things were going from bad to worse. God alone knew what horrible new misadventures would happen if the Vane family remained with them for that long. He made his excuses and took a hurried leave, wondering how this was all going to turn out and seriously doubting that his future mother-in-law could go a whole six weeks without bringing up the subject of mumps.

Chapter Nine

Mrs. Vane was ecstatic about the family's invitation to Fairhaven. Her younger daughter was not. "The season is not over," complained Elyza. "How will I make this grand match you expect if you take me away from London before the season is even over and board me up for weeks?"

"My dear girl," said her mother patiently. "We shall let it be known where we are going, so your suitors will know well enough how to find you. And furthermore, I am sure Viscountess Fairwood will invite other guests besides ourselves, since that is often the custom." Mrs. Vane smiled as a pleasant vision danced before her eyes. "You never know whom you may meet at a house party. And, I assure you, my darling, many a match has been made at just such a gathering."

"Not the one I want," muttered Elyza.

"What?" said her mother sharply.

"Nothing, Mama," said Elyza meekly.

Having swept aside her daughter's objections, Mrs. Vane now proceeded forward with her preparations at a rapid speed. An enthusiastic note was sent to Lady Fairwood, telling her how very thrilled they all were with her kind offer, letting her know their proposed time of arrival, and hinting broadly that it wouldn't be found objectionable if she provided some other houseguests, as well, in the form of handsome young suitors for Mrs. Vane's younger daughter.

The day before their departure the trunks had been packed and repacked, everyone of importance had been notified of the Vane family's departure for Gloucestershire—many of whom had breathed a sigh of relief—and the servants had been given their instructions. All preparations had gone smoothly and everything was in readiness.

And after all this preparation, Mrs. Vane took it as an insult to her efficiency that her husband should manage to contract a cold and a putrid sore throat. "Mr. Vane, how could you?" she lamented, standing by her fevered husband's bedside. "Now we shall have to postpone our visit."

"I won't hear of it," rasped her husband. "You must go on without me, my dear. I shall join you when I am better."

His wife looked shocked. "We cannot leave you alone in a big silent house when you are ill."

If Mr. Vane thought it a wonderful idea to be left to recover in peace, and with the house to himself, he was wise enough not to say so. He merely shook his fevered head. "This is your moment of triumph, my dear, and I wouldn't dream of taking it from you. Besides, did I not hear you say what a wonderful opportunity it would be for Elyza to meet someone suitable? Surely you would not deprive her of so much as a day of such opportunity." Mr. Vane punctuated this last sentence with a sneeze, moaned, and lay back amongst the bed pillows.

"Oh, dear," fretted his wife.

"I shall be fine in a week or two," insisted her husband. "We must think of the children."

"Yes, that is true," said Mrs. Vane, determination strengthening her resolve. "We shall go. But I will leave instructions with Dodders that he send for us immediately if you should take a turn for the worse. And I shall have Cook make you some chicken broth directly."

"Thank you," said her husband, then closed his eyes and smiled.

Charles accompanied the ladies to his ancestral home, and except for the fact that her stepsister insisted on flirting with him, Emily found the journey an enjoyable one. Her bogus fiancé was good company, and kept them entertained with bits of information about the shires they passed through.

"You are better than a guide book," Emily told him, and he smiled.

"If one likes that sort of thing," said Elyza with a yawn.

"Tell us more about Fairhaven," prompted Emily.

Charles obliged, sharing anecdotes about the various neighbors, and incidents from his boyhood.

"I am sure every woman for miles set her cap for you," said Elyza, giving him a teasing look.

Charles shrugged. "A few, perhaps," he said modestly. "The one my mother wanted for me was Miss Bromwell. Little Betty Bromwell, as my mother calls her." He shook his head. "I am afraid the only thing little about Miss Bromwell is the amount of space left for another person on the sofa once she is seated there."

Elyza giggled. Mrs. Vane smiled tolerantly. Emily found it hard to smile.

Charles cocked his head at her. "You disapprove of my jest?" he asked.

Emily looked out the carriage window. "Having never been beautiful myself, I suppose I find it hard to see any humor in the poor fortune of a person born less lovely than others."

"Emily!" scolded her stepmama. "Don't be ridiculous. There is nothing in the least wrong with the way you look. Of course, you are not as beautiful as Elyza, but to talk as if you are less than acceptable is most ridiculous."

Charles looked at Emily's pink face and lowered eyes and felt an odd tenderness. "You ain't so bad to look at, Emily," he said softly. "At least, I don't think so."

She raised her eyes to his and the grateful look he saw in them made him feel suddenly as if he were a knight who had rescued a lady from a fire-breathing dragon. He smiled encouragingly at her and she smiled back.

She really was a good sort, he mused. And she deserved better than to be caught in a mess like this. He hoped when it was all over, she found some nice man to marry her. And not that rake, Beddington! Maybe his mother could help him think of someone suitable for Emily. He certainly couldn't think of anyone worthy of her right off. But then, women were better at that sort of thing. His mother was bound to think of someone. And on that pleasant note, Charles allowed himself to relax his mind and believe that, somehow, things would all work out and he would be able to marry his heart's desire.

* * *

The Vane ladies and Charles arrived at his home at just the right time of day. The afternoon sun shone on Fairhaven Manor, revealing it in all its rambling splendour, and actually causing Mrs. Vane to catch her breath and be silent for a good moment before bursting into raptures.

The viscountess welcomed the newcomers and instructed the butler to have them shown to their rooms to freshen up with a promise of having tea awaiting them in the drawing room. "For travelling can be so fatiguing. And, naturally, we are most anxious to have the opportunity for a nice, comfortable coze with Charles's intended." She smiled kindly on Emily, who murmured a polite thank-you.

"So very kind," gushed Mrs. Vane. She beamed on Charles. "I must say that Charles made a very good choice when he offered for our Emily. Such a good girl. She will make a charming viscountess some day, I am sure."

Lady Fairwood stiffened at this speech, but Mrs. Vane took no notice, rambling on, "And we are all atwitter to see more of your lovely home. Charles told me you have been redecorating. I am sure it is all in the first stare of elegance. I, myself, have wanted to refurbish our home for the longest time, but I am afraid Mr. Vane is terribly clutch-fisted when it comes to that sort of thing." She took Lady Fairwood by the arm as if they were bosom beaus. "We shall have to put our heads together and see if we can change his mind."

"Er, yes," said Lady Fairwood. She gently disengaged her arm from Mrs. Vane's grasp. "Addison will take you up now. I am sure you are most anxious to freshen up."

"Yes," agreed Mrs. Vane. "Travelling is such dirty work, no matter how careful one is. Come, girls," she said, and followed the butler up one side of the split staircase.

Charles made to slink off, but his mother's voice stopped him. "Charles, perhaps you could give me a moment of your time before changing?"

Charles bit his lip and followed his mother into the drawing room.

The door was barely shut before she turned an accusing look on him and demanded, "*Where* did you find that odious woman!"

Charles shrugged helplessly. "She came with Emily," he said.

"Really, Charles. How could you have been so thoughtless as to become engaged to a girl with a mother like that? Whatever were you thinking of?"

A vision of Elyza's delicate curves and perfect face came to mind. One could hardly tell one's mother about that. "I don't know," he said lamely. "But you will like Emily," he offered.

"She had best be a paragon," warned Lady Fairwood. "For nothing short of it will compensate for having such a mother."

Charles made good his escape and went to his room to change. This gathering made a mockery of the words, *house party*, and he was sure the next few weeks would be the longest in his life.

With everyone changed and freshened, the two families met in the drawing room for tea. Mrs. Vane looked at the swirling dragons on the wall and nodded approvingly. "I vow I have not seen anything so elegant in any drawing room in London," she said. "What excellent taste my Lady has."

This comment didn't necessarily raise Lady Fairwood's opinion of Mrs. Vane, but it reinforced her high opinion of her artistic gift for decorating and she smiled. "I am pleased with it," she said modestly.

Her husband merely grunted. Mrs. Vane gave him a playful smile and announced that husbands were all the same.

Lady Fairwood changed the subject. "We are so sorry your husband could not be with us."

"And he sends his deepest regrets," said Mrs. Vane. "Such an inconvenient time to be indisposed! I know he was very much looking forward to meeting you, Lord Fairwood."

"Perhaps he will be feeling better in time to join us later," suggested Lady Fairwood politely. "Meanwhile, we hope you will enjoy your stay," she said. "We thought, perhaps, a ball in honor of the betrothed couple would be in order."

"Oh, yes," agreed Mrs. Vane enthusiastically. Now she turned her playful look on Lady Fairwood. "And I am sure my dear Elyza would not object if you were to invite a great many eligible young men from good families."

Lady Fairwood stiffly assured her there would be a good number of eligible parties present.

"How delightful!" enthused Mrs. Vane. "I should be happy to help you make out the invitations tomorrow. It would be so exciting to find husbands for both girls in one season, for I can assure you that the cost of a London season has put a terrific strain upon my husband's purse, and I fear what he might say if Elyza does not secure a husband and he must face it all again next spring. Of course, no sacrifice is too much for my daughters," she continued. "It is terribly exhausting, rushing from one social obligation to another, but never let it be said that the Vane ladies did not take because their mama was unwilling to do her part."

Emily blushed as her stepmother rambled on. She had seen the forced smile on Lady Fairwood's face. She had also seen the viscount's eyebrow raise a time or two. Mrs. Vane paused to take a breath and Emily bravely inserted herself into the conversation. "This is a wonderful seed cake," she ventured.

"Oh, yes," gushed Mrs. Vane. "I do hope I can impose on you to give me the recipe for our cook. Never have I eaten such a delicious seed cake! And I have a recipe, which I am sure you would be delighted to have. It is for the Prince Regent's own punch. I had it from my dear cousin, Lady Runcible. Perhaps you are acquainted with Lady Runcible? Oh, but I am sure you must be, for anyone who is anyone knows Lady Runcible!"

Emily gave up. There was no way she could stop her stepmama from embarrassing them all. She sent Charles a look of apology, and he rolled his eyes and shrugged.

His sister, Gwendolyn, had been stealing looks at the beautiful Elyza the entire time. Now she ventured to speak to the glorious creature. "We have a pretty stream running along the edge of our property. Perhaps you would care to go on a picnic there."

Elyza cast a coy look in Charles's direction. "That sounds most romantic," she said sweetly.

Charles blushed and smiled at her, and Emily sighed inwardly. Then she heard what her stepmother was saying and experienced yet another emotion.

"We are glad your family is finally over their siege with the mumps," said Mrs. Vane. "Nasty business," she continued. "I can see why you did not wish your son exposed."

Mrs. Trevor looked questioningly at her son.

Charles was mercifully spared, for at that moment the nurse made her appearance with little Phillip. In spite of his nurse's warnings to behave himself like a proper young gentleman of five years and walk when entering the room and not to speak unless he was spoken to, Phillip made his entrance in an excited rush.

On his way to his brother, he managed to trample Elyza's toes, bringing a cry of pain from the beauty.

"Oh, dear!" cried her mama. "Are they broken?"

"Mama, I don't think the weight of a small child would be enough to break Elyza's toes," remonstrated Emily gently.

"How would you know?" retorted her stepsister. "It was not your foot that was trod upon."

"Phillip!" scolded Charles. "Why the devil don't you watch where you are going?"

"Now, Charles. Don't scold," said his mama. "It was an accident, and we can always forgive an accident. Can we not, Miss Vane?"

Elyza erased the scowl from her face and said what was proper, and her mother beamed approvingly on her.

"Well, now, Phillip," said his father. "What do you say to the lady?"

Phillip looked at Elyza. "Do you like to play at spillikins?" he asked.

The company laughed and Elyza smiled but conveniently forgot to reply.

"I like to play at spillikins," offered Emily.

Phillip's face lit up. "Do you?" he cried. "Will you play with me?"

"Of course," said Emily.

"And will you, Charles?"

"Yes, pest," said Charles tolerantly. "I will."

"Will the pretty lady play, too?" asked Phillip.

"Of course, she will," said Mrs. Vane.

Elyza looked at her mother in amazement, but feeling all eyes on herself, schooled her face into pleasant lines and nodded.

Later, as she sat at her dressing table, watching her abigail put the finishing touches on her toilette, she announced that she intended to stay as far away from the horrid little boy as possible. Even as she spoke, she caught sight of movement by her bed, and realized it was none other than the horrid little boy, himself. "What are you doing here?" she cried. "Get out!"

Phillip scampered out of the room, slamming the door behind him and ran straight into Emily, who was coming down the hall.

He nearly knocked her over, but she recovered herself enough to regain her balance, and ask, "Why the hurry, Master Phillip?"

"I have to get back to Nurse," he said.

Emily nodded seriously. "I am sure she is getting lonely."

"Nurse loves me," said Phillip.

"I am sure she does," agreed Emily. She smiled at the boy. "May I walk with you?"

"Are you going to play spillikins with me now?" asked Phillip hopefully, starting off down the hall.

"Well, not right now," said Emily, falling in step with him. "I must go and have dinner with the grown-ups. But I do want to play."

Phillip smiled up at her. "I don't like the pretty lady," he announced. "But I like you."

"I like you, also, Phillip," she said.

She returned Phillip to the grateful arms of his nurse and went down to dinner. The Trevor family kept a good table, offering their guests everything from fine turtle soup to Italian sausage and Turkish figs and dates. The second course alone contained twenty-five dishes.

As two footmen went around the table with various dishes, Emily stole a look at her stepsister. Elyza was wearing the kind of speculative look on her face that boded mischief. What was she up to now!

Emily learned soon enough later that night. Her sister paid her a visit after Emily dismissed her maid. "You have certainly landed in clover," Elyza informed her. She looked around at Emily's bedroom. "This room is much finer than mine."

"All the rooms, I am sure, are lovely," said Emily.

"Oh, they are," agreed Elyza. "I could be happy in such a house."

Emily understood the meaning of that statement. "There are many houses finer than this in England," she said.

Elyza smiled wickedly. "And so, dear sister, please do not steal my treasure from me," she said in a pitiful voice, her face pleading. The expression quickly changed to one of hauteur. "Charles should have been mine, and well we both know it."

"There is nothing you can do about that now," retorted Emily.

Elyza smiled slyly. "Oh? Is there not?"

"You'd best not try any of your tricks," cautioned Emily. She brought out her only weapon against her sister. "Mama would not be happy, I assure you."

"Pish posh," said Elyza, flinging aside this remonstrance with a flick of her hand.

Suddenly, Emily realized she had no desire to release Charles from their engagement just so her selfish little sister could have him. "You can do better than Charles," she suggested.

"I could have, if you had not meddled," snapped Elyza. "I could have been engaged to Beddington by now but for you. Well, I shall be engaged before the month is out, and I shall take great pleasure in pulling your catch right out of your net." With that she marched out of the room.

Emily ground her teeth. "We'll just see about that," she muttered.

It was one thing for Elyza to make off with her favorite hair ribbons, to borrow her gloves and never return them, to pout whenever Emily got a new gown until she had one, too. And it was one thing for her stepsister to reach out with greedy hands and pull every man who ever even smiled at Emily into her own large circle of admirers. But to steal Charles? No, never!

And she wasn't being selfish in wanting him for herself. He would never be happy with Elyza. Oh, he might think he would. But Elyza was selfish and spoilt and sneaky. And besides, she would tire of him within a month. No. It would not do to let Elyza steal him away. He would be miserable in the end. She had to fight Elyza for him. For his own good.

The next morning Elyza broke a long-standing tradition, and was the first one up. She was directed to the small parlor the family used for breakfast, and found Lady Fairwood there alone. The viscountess asked her how she slept and she smiled sweetly and replied that she had slept very well. "The room you have put me in is so lovely, I am quite comfortable in it."

Lady Fairwood smiled, gratified. "I am glad you slept well," she said.

"You have such a lovely home here, my Lady," continued Elyza sweetly. "And such a dear family. It is a pity Papa could not come with us to meet them." She sighed.

"We were sorry to hear he is indisposed," said Lady Fairwood politely.

"Of course, it is to be expected," said Elyza. "Papa is always melancholy this time of year."

"There is so much rain," agreed the viscountess.

"Oh, it is not that," said Elyza. "It was around this time of year when he lost his first wife." She looked suddenly embarrassed. "Oh, dear, I should not have said anything."

"My dear child, we are soon to be family," the older woman pointed out. "Surely there is no need for any reticence on your part."

"I suppose you would be told sooner or later. Would you not?"

Lady Fairwood nodded encouragingly.

Elyza looked at her lap. "Papa still grieves for his first wife. It has been some years since she went ma—er, to her reward."

Lady Fairwood was neither stupid, nor was her hearing at all impaired. "Mad? Were you about to say mad?" she asked sharply.

"She is dead now," said Elyza earnestly.

"But before she died. . . . She went mad?"

Elyza nodded her head, the picture of shame. "She died shortly after. And then Papa met my mama, and things have been fine ever since. It is only at this time of year he remembers. But he has Emily to comfort him. She bears a great resemblance to her mother. Papa has a great fondness for her, which is why he was so happy to see her find someone at last. You know how people can be when there is madness in the family."

"Of course," said the viscountess weakly. She set down her tea cup and excused herself, rushing off to find her husband.

Elyza leisurely finished her breakfast, then strolled outside into the rose garden. It was here that fate once more played into her hand, sending Charles ambling by. "Elyza! You are up and about early," he said, coming to join her on a little stone bench.

"I was just enjoying your lovely garden," she said, her pitiful expression belying her words.

"You don't look much as if you were enjoying it," said Charles.

"Oh, I was. Truly. But I was also thinking how strange life is. How different my life might have been if Mama had not expected me to make a grand match with Lord Beddington."

Charles looked at Elyza in amazement. "She did? Didn't she know Beddington's reputation?"

Elyza shrugged. "I suppose she thought he must settle sometime. She wished me to encourage him so I could make a grand match. But really, my heart was already fixed on someone else." Here she stole a shy glance at Charles. She met his eyes only long enough to see the hope in them, then lowered her gaze. "I am afraid I have sadly misspent my London season," she confessed. "To encourage a man like Lord Beddington when I wanted another. . . ." She raised her grief-stricken face to Charles. Her lower lip began to tremble and she searched Charles's eyes. "Oh, Charles," she cried, "I am afraid my life is ruined." With that announcement, she burst into tears and turned her face into his shoulder.

At this moment Emily happened to look out a window and see the touching scene in the garden. She saw Charles's arm creep up around Elyza. So. The battle for Charles had begun in earnest. "You will not have him without a fight," she vowed softly.

Lord Fairwood also happened to be looking out the window of his library. He had not the same advantageous view of the garden as Emily, but he could see some of it. He could see the little stone bench where his son sat with his arm around the woman to whom he was not betrothed.

A look of extreme irritation crossed his face and his wife, misinterpreting it, fretted, "Oh, dear. Then you think it true?"

"Of course not," said the viscount. "Such nonsense!" he declared. "Sounds like a tale from the Minerva Press."

"Why should the child lie?" countered Lady Fairwood.

"Why, indeed?" he asked, turning to look at his wife. "You are a woman. You tell me."

Lady Fairwood looked at her husband. Her eyes narrowed and she nodded. "Yes," she said slowly. "Why, indeed?"

She left her husband and went straight to her bedroom, where she sat down at her escritoire and penned a note to her second cousin, who claimed some knowledge of the Vane family. ". . . . Anything you can discover, my dear Elizabeth, will be greatly appreciated." Lady Fairwood brushed her chin with the feather of her quill. What if Miss Elyza Vane had spoken the truth? Yet her stepsister seemed perfectly normal. Ah, but with madness one never knew. It could come on so suddenly.

A canker on the brain and ... Lady Fairwood bit her lip. Her poor, dear son. Well, she would soon get to the bottom of this. And if there were madness in the family, they would simply have to find someone else to marry the girl.

Chapter Ten

As soon as his wife left him, Lord Fairwood decided he needed a break from his work and that a stroll in the garden would be in order. His son was still there, consoling the beautiful Miss Vane. "Charles," said the older man in a strong voice, and the guilty pair jumped apart.

"Father," said Charles, his face flushing hotly.

"It is a fine morning. Perhaps our guests would care for a ride about the estate," suggested the viscount, looking sternly at Elyza.

"That would be very nice," said Elyza. "I shall just go put on my riding habit."

Casting a nervous glance at the viscount, she made good her escape and Lord Fairwood levelled his gaze on his son.

"Father," began Charles.

"I know she is a pretty thing," he began. "But I'll not have you playing fast and loose under my roof, my boy. It is one thing to set up a bit of muslin in the proper part of town, but it is quite another to carry on with one female when you are engaged to her sister. Your mother would be scandalized and I'll not have it."

"But I wasn't carrying on with her," protested Charles. "I was comforting her."

"Leave that to her mother," said the viscount, heading back to the house. "And take your sister riding, too. Perhaps her presence will protect you from any further 'chivalrous' urges."

Charles sighed and followed his father. Really, it had not been at all what it looked, he reasoned self-righteously, forgetting how close he had come to kissing those sweet lips, which, for one tempting moment, had hovered so near his.

Elyza met her sister in the hallway. "We are to go riding and see the estate," she said. "I was just now on my way to tell you."

Emily decided to pretend she hadn't witnessed the scene in the garden. "That will be nice," she replied, trying to make her voice sound normal.

Elyza smiled, catlike. "Yes, won't it?"

When Elyza returned downstairs, she discovered that not only was Emily to be riding with them, but Gwendolyn as well. "Papa suggested I might like to go along," said Gwendolyn, admiration shining in her eyes.

"What a good idea," said Elyza silkily. "Three is such an awkward number. Four is much better. That way no one need feel left out."

Emily listened to this little speech and knew exactly who her stepsister envisioned talking with Gwendolyn. She tried not to let it sour her spirit, reminding herself that she liked the girl. If she wound up next to her for most of the ride, it would not be so bad.

But the one who wound up next to Gwendolyn for most of the ride was Elyza, for his father's stern words were fresh in Charles's mind, and much as he might like to have spent a pleasant two hours flirting with the beautiful girl, he also wished to keep his head firmly on his shoulders rather than have it roared off by an angry parent. And it wasn't so very painful riding next to Emily, he decided. "You really are a good sort," he told her.

Emily smiled, pleased. "Thank you," she said. "It is good of you to say so."

"No, no. I am not making up some compliment just for something to say," said Charles.

"You certainly don't need to," Emily assured him.

"I know it, and that is why I said what I did. Most females would be chattering away, saying silly things, fishing for compliments about their hat, or their hair, or how well they look sitting a horse. You don't do that."

"We did not ride out to see my hat," said Emily. "We rode out to see the estate. And it is lovely, Charles," she added, eyes shining. "I can see you are well liked by all your tenants."

Charles shrugged in embarrassment. "You know how it is. They have all known me since I was in leading strings."

"That doesn't mean they must like you."

"They seem to like you, too," said Charles.

Emily smiled at him. "It is because I am with you."

Meanwhile, Gwendolyn was attempting to pump Elyza about the London social whirl. "Did you go to many parties?" she asked.

"A good many," said Elyza.

"How wonderful it must be," sighed Gwendolyn.

"It is if you are beautiful," said Elyza. "If you are not, the gentlemen don't pay you much attention."

"You must have had many suitors," observed Gwendolyn.

Elyza nodded and shrugged indifferently. "The only

reason I am not yet engaged is because I cannot make up my mind among them."

"And I suppose you had to wait until Emily was engaged," offered Gwendolyn.

"Yes," said Elyza. "Charles was one of my admirers. Emily tricked him into offering for her."

Gwendolyn's eyes grew wide. "She tricked him?"

Elyza nodded. "Poor Charles. If Emily had not served him such a dirty trick, I daresay he would have been engaged to me. I would have been the one riding next to him, seeing the estate, meeting the tenants." She sighed.

"Do you love him?" asked Gwendolyn earnestly.

"What can it matter now?" replied Elyza, looking tragic. "We are lost, and all because of a selfish sister. Ah, Gwendolyn. Be glad you only have brothers."

Gwendolyn could hardly contain herself for the rest of the ride. As soon as they had walked back from the stables and the Vane sisters had gone to their rooms to change, she drew her brother off to the nearest saloon and shut the door. "Charles! What shall we do?" she cried, throwing herself into his arms.

"Here now," said Charles. "What are you doing to my coat, Gwen?"

"Oh, never mind your silly coat," she said. "And you don't need to pretend with me. Elyza told me all. I know your heart is breaking."

Charles stared at his sister. "What, exactly, did Elyza tell you?" he asked.

"Why, how you were both in love, but Emily tricked you into marrying her. What a wicked thing to do! And she seems so nice."

"She is nice," said Charles sternly. "And I'll not hear anybody say she ain't."

"But she tricked you," protested Gwendolyn.

"She didn't trick me. It was, er, an accident," said Charles.

"An accident! What can you mean?"

"Never mind," said her brother testily. "And don't you go repeating that cockeyed story or you'll have us all in the soup. Tricked me, indeed."

"But it is Elyza you wanted to marry," continued his little sister.

Charles scratched his head. "Well, there's no denying that. But it ain't all the great tragedy you are making it. In fact, things will most likely turn out fine," he finished comfortingly.

"I don't see how you can say that when you cannot marry the woman you love," said his sister in tragic accents.

Charles could hardly tell her about Emily's scheme to end their engagement. With Gwen's loose lips, the whole sorry story would be all over the shire before the cat could lick its ear. "Don't worry so, Gwen," he said and gave his sister's nose a tweak. "Let those of us who know what we are doing handle the ribbons."

"It doesn't seem to me that someone who accidentally got himself engaged to one woman when he wanted another can know what he is doing at all," muttered Gwendolyn.

Her brother told her to keep her nose on her face where it belonged instead of poking it into other people's business and made his exit.

Gwendolyn sighed. How very perplexing life was when one was out! She wandered off in search of her mama, and found Lady Fairwood with Mrs. Vane, fully absorbed in addressing invitations for a ball to be held in two weeks' time. Suddenly the strange behavior of her brother and the Misses Vane was forgotten. "Oh, Mama. May I attend? Please?"

"Certainly not," said her mother firmly. "A small dinner party is one thing, but a ball is quite another. Besides, darling, it will not be such a grand affair, so quickly thrown together as it is—just a few of the neighbors in to meet Charles's intended."

"Oh, but Mama, if it is to be such a small, poor affair as you say, then surely it cannot matter if I am present."

"You must listen to your mama," advised Mrs. Vane in playful tones. "For Mamas always know what is best for their daughters."

"Oh, but Mrs. Vane, surely you let your daughters attend small parties before they were out. With Elyza so beautiful, I am sure she could not wait to be properly out."

"Well, I suppose I did indulge her a little," admitted Mrs. Vane. "And if it is to be a small affair, perhaps we should let her attend."

Lady Fairwood smiled stiffly and said, "We shall see."

The family kept country hours, and family and guests gathered for dinner at five o'clock. Emily found herself seated between Lady Fairwood and her stepsister.

"Did you enjoy your ride this morning?" asked Lady Fairwood.

"Oh, yes," said Emily. "I do love the country."

"It is very nice here," agreed the viscountess. "I am afraid it must seem slow after the social whirl in London."

"I believe I prefer a slower pace," said Emily. "It seems the last few weeks have been so full we have barely had time to sleep. I thought I should go mad with all the activity."

Lady Fairwood choked on her soup, and Elyza looked innocently at her plate.

Emily looked at the viscountess with concern and wondered what she could have said to so upset that good woman. How very odd, indeed!

The rest of the evening passed without incident, the company amusing themselves at the pianoforte, then visiting until the supper tray arrived. That is, Mrs. Vane visited. Lady Fairwood sat with a polite smile pinned on her face, occasionally stifling a yawn.

"That woman does not wear well," observed Lord Fairwood, when he came to visit his wife later that night.

"No, she does not," agreed Lady Fairwood. "Why Charles could not have chosen more carefully I do not know."

"After having seen the daughter, I do," said the viscount. "Ah, my dear, I would not be young again for all the world."

Emily wouldn't have agreed with the viscount if she'd been privy to his conversation, for youth was hope. After her enjoyable ride with Charles, she took pleasant dreams to bed with her. Charles did like her. Perhaps, if he grew to like her enough, it would blossom into something more.

The next day was gray and drizzly, and the company found themselves trapped within doors. After luncheon, Emily suggested a visit to little Phillip in the nursery. "We did promise to play spillikins with him," she reminded Charles.

"I shall come, too," said Gwendolyn. She turned to Elyza. "Will you join us, Elyza?"

"Of course," said Elyza. She smiled coyly at Charles. "I shall enjoy playing with Charles."

They made their way to the wing where Miss Stubbin, the family's nurse for the past twenty years, reigned supreme, and found Phillip in the middle of consuming scones and jam.

"Charles," he cried, and without bothering to wipe the jam from either fingers or face, ignored the remonstrances of his nurse and ran on stubby little legs to his big brother, who had come in after the ladies.

Tripping in his haste, he reached out and grabbed for support. What his clutching fingers found was Elyza's gown.

Nearly toppled, she squealed. Charles reached out a steadying arm and stopped her from going over, and she looked gratefully up at him, rewarding him with a smile. Then she looked down at her gown and the smile fell from her face. "My gown!" she gasped. "Oh, look at it. It is quite ruined!"

"Oh, dear!" cried Gwendolyn.

Elyza made a sound of disgust. "Look what you have done, you clumsy little boy," she scolded the child.

Charles pulled out his handkerchief. "Here, perhaps we can—"

"No!" commanded Elyza. "You will only make it worse. I shall have to go change at once."

Little Phillip's mouth was trembling. A fat tear tumbled down his cheek.

Emily bent kindly over him. "Now, there is no need to cry," she said gently. "It is, after all, only a gown."

"Oh, that is easy for you to say," retorted Elyza. "It is not your gown that was ruined."

Little Phillip looked to Emily, his eyes tragic.

Emily said nothing. She marched to where the tray of scones sat and scooped up the pot of jam. There was a chorus of gasps as she held out her gown and emptied the contents of the pot on it. Emily smiled at Phillip, who clapped his hands and laughed. She turned and scraped the jam back into the pot as best she could, saying, "You see? It is not such a terrible thing to have jam on your gown." She licked her finger and smiled as her stepsister tossed her head and left the room with a haughty snort.

"Why did you do such a thing?" asked Gwendolyn, finding her voice at last.

Emily strolled back to rejoin the group at the door. "Because gowns are expendable. Feelings are not." She looked down at Phillip. "But it is a little difficult to play spillikins when one is all sticky. I shall go change gowns and be back in a trice."

Gwendolyn turned to her older brother after Emily had left the room. "What an amazing lady," she said.

"Pretty is as pretty does, my mother used to say," murmured Miss Stubbin. "And how right she was."

Charles said nothing, but the difference in behavior between the two sisters was not lost on him.

Emily returned twenty minutes later, in time to get in on a rousing game of spillikins. They progressed from that to hide-and-seek, and became so engrossed in their play, they nearly failed to hear the gong for dinner.

Charles looked at Emily's dusty gown and shook his head. "You have managed to ruin two gowns in one day," he told her.

"Oh, I don't care," she said. "I had great fun."

Charles smiled. "I did, too." He cocked his head. "Do

you know? You are better company than any female I met in London," he said.

"Yes," piped in Phillip. "I like Emily," he added, taking Emily's hand.

"And I like you, too," she said, squeezing the little hand.

"Stay here and have dinner with Nurse and me," offered Phillip.

"You've seen enough of Emily today," said Charles firmly. "And we have seen enough of you."

"Will you play with me tomorrow?" asked Phillip.

"We shall see," Charles answered for her, holding the door open. "Come on, girls. We had better hurry or mother will have the footmen looking for us."

Emily bid her new friend farewell and went to her room to dress for dinner. She encountered the little boy's distraught nurse later when she stepped out of her room. It seemed that Master Phillip had managed to give the poor woman the slip.

"I am so sorry to bother you, Miss Vane, but I thought, perhaps, he might have come to see you," said Miss Stubbin. "He took such a shine to you."

"I have not seen him," said Emily. "The sun has come out. Perhaps he slipped outside."

The woman nodded. "He has, most likely, gone out into the garden."

"I do hope you find him," said Emily, and hurried down the stairs to the drawing room.

It was another quiet family evening, but Lady Fairwood announced that she had invited company for the following evening. "It will be a small gathering— just Lord and Lady Livingstone, the Bromwells and their daughter, Betty . . ."

At the mention of the worthy young lady Charles's mama had wanted for him, Emily looked at Charles. He rolled his eyes expressively, and Emily almost giggled.

"Lord and Lady Livingstone have a houseguest with them whom they will be bringing," the viscountess was saying. Here she turned to Mrs. Vane. "I believe he is quite an eligible man. Titled, too. And the Bromwells will bring their son, Edward, and his friend, Captain Fawley, who is also a personable young man."

Charles made a face of disgust and Emily smiled. Captain Fawley must be a dandy, she thought.

"And I believe we might get up some dancing for the young people after dinner," added Lady Fairwood.

Mrs. Vane pronounced this a very good idea, indeed, and was still giving Lady Fairwood ideas on how to ensure a successful evening when the ladies settled themselves in the drawing room.

Gwendolyn sighed and wished she was out. "How I should like to attend the dinner party," she said, "but Mama is such a stickler."

"I doubt you shall miss much," said Elyza. "It will be, most likely, merely a collection of country nobodies."

Just what did her stepsister think they were? Emily shot a quick glance in Lady Fairwood's direction, hoping she hadn't heard Elyza's ungrateful comment.

"Lord and Lady Livingstone are very important people," Gwendolyn assured Elyza. "And I believe the guest who has just come to them is also important. I don't remember his name, but he is an earl. And Captain Fawley is very handsome. He is, in fact, the most handsome man I have ever seen." Gwendolyn's expression turned dreamy. "I saw him once in his regimentals, and I shall never forget the sight." She sighed. "He picked me a rose. I have it still, pressed between the pages of *The Mutual Attachment*."

"So, what do you think this Captain Fawley might be like?" asked Elyza later that night, as she lay across her sister's bed, watching Foster unpin Emily's hair.

Emily shrugged. "He sounds very intriguing."

Elyza rolled onto her back and began swinging her legs over the side of the bed. "And the other gentleman?"

"He sounds a finer catch," said Emily.

"So I thought," said Elyza. "If he is as wonderful as Gwendolyn says, perhaps I shall take him. Then you may keep Charles after all."

"The way you have been behaving I doubt he will want you anymore, anyway," said Emily.

"Don't be silly," said her sister. "He should have to be blind not to want me." She sat up and hopped off the bed. "Ah, well. We shall see what tomorrow brings. Goodnight."

Foster said nothing but continued to unpin her mistress's hair.

"I know," said Emily. "She is a sad trial. Perhaps someday she will meet someone as beautiful as herself."

"That would give her a bit of her own medicine," muttered Foster, and Emily did not rebuke her.

Elyza had only been gone to her own room for a few minutes when her shriek reached Emily's ears. "Good heavens!" cried Emily, throwing on her wrapper. "What can have happened?" She tore to the room next door, Foster behind her.

There stood Elyza, hands on hips, a scowl on her face, watching as her maid scurried about the room trying bravely to scoop up a little, green tree frog which she obviously had no desire to touch. "Look at that!"

declared Elyza, pointing to the frightened frog. "I opened my jewel box to put away my necklace and that—thing—hopped out. It nearly frightened me out of my wits."

Lord and Lady Fairwood and Charles had now come on the scene as well. Charles rushed into the room, and scooped up the frog. "A present from Phillip?" he guessed.

Elyza shut her eyes and drew in a deep breath, looking like the world's most beautiful martyr.

Now Mrs. Vane made her appearance on the scene. "Elyza, my child!" she cried, running to her daughter's side. "What has happened here?" She looked accusingly at Charles, as if some ungentlemanly behavior on his part were the cause of her daughter's scream.

He held out his hands and uncupped them to show her the frog. With the prison doors swung free, the poor thing jumped for freedom, causing fresh shrieks and pandemonium. The frog was finally captured and Charles made his exit.

"Phillip shall be made to apologize to you first thing in the morning," Lady Fairwood assured Elyza. "I cannot imagine why he would do such a naughty thing."

"I wonder," said Emily, looking accusingly at her sister.

Elyza's chin came up and her eyes narrowed, but she said nothing.

"I shall have cook brew you a tisane to help you sleep," Lady Fairwood said.

"Thank you," Elyza murmured.

"Well, now," said the viscount. "I suggest we all find our beds."

Neither Emily nor Foster said anything all the way back to Emily's room. Not a word was said once the door was shut. But anyone passing by Emily's door a short minute later would have heard what sounded suspiciously like laughter.

The next day Emily noticed that her stepsister was spending an amazing amount of her afternoon getting ready for what she had predicted would only be a gathering of country nobodies.

"Where is your sister?" Charles asked as they rambled through the garden, enjoying the sunshine.

"Trying on gowns, I imagine," Emily replied. Charles looked at her uncomprehendingly. "She wants to look her best for the party tonight," Emily explained.

"And she needs all day to do that?"

Emily considered. "Yes, I believe she does. There is so much to do. A lady must decide what gown she is going to wear, and once she has decided on that, she must find gloves to go with it, and something to wear in her hair. Then, of course, she must rest in order to look fresh . . ."

Charles made a sound of disgust.

"Come now," teased Emily. "You aren't going to tell me you don't spend a great deal of time in choosing a waistcoat or in tying a cravat."

"Of course I spend a great deal of time," agreed Charles. "But it don't take me all afternoon."

"You are not a great beauty with a reputation to maintain," pointed out Emily.

"Well, thank God I am not," said Charles heartily. "And thank God you don't consider yourself one, either, Emily, for who should I have to talk with if you were like Elyza and holed up in your room all day?"

Emily sighed. "No, there is no danger of me considering myself a great beauty," she said wistfully.

Charles looked at her, and seeing the sadness in her

eyes, said, "You shouldn't let it blue devil you that you ain't as pretty as your sister."

"Oh, it doesn't bother me so very much," said Emily, trying to sound cheerful. "After all, we cannot all be beautiful. Although sometimes I wonder why," she added under her breath.

Charles laughed at this. "I can tell you why," he said. "If we were all as beautiful as your sister, we should all spend the day in our rooms, prancing before the looking glass, seeing no one and doing nothing, and that would be the devil of a bore!"

Emily was pleased with this. "You are a very witty man," she observed.

"Me?" said Charles in surprise.

"I think you are," she said, her cheeks turning pink.

Charles grinned. "Cleverness runs in my family," he said, and Emily giggled, knowing exactly to whom he was alluding.

"Poor Phillip," she said. "I do hope your mama did not scold him too much."

"Well, she did prose on about how one cannot go about putting frogs in people's jewel boxes simply because they ain't nice. Anyway, I guess he said his apology all right and tight. He told me that father gave him a sugarplum afterward."

Emily was able to repress a giggle, but it was impossible to hold down a smile.

"Emily! You have a dimple," observed Charles in amazement. Emily blushed scarlet, but he didn't notice, so caught up was he in digesting this new discovery. "I wonder I never noticed it before," he said and shook his head. "I rather like dimples," he confessed, then turned a shade of pink himself. His eyes fell on a lilac bush in full bloom. "Do you like these?" he asked. Emily nodded, and he broke off a spray of lilacs and handed it to her.

"Thank you," she said. "I shall have Foster put this in water so I may wear it in my hair tonight."

Charles smiled, and the two strolled back to the house in comfortable silence.

When Elyza made her appearance for the dinner party it was apparent her afternoon had not been wasted. She was a vision in a gown of pink watered silk. A pearl necklace hung about her throat and pearl droplets dangled from her tiny ears.

Emily looked at her stepsister and felt dowdy in the lavender gown she had chosen. The flowers in her hair were nothing compared to the little pearl clips so cleverly inserted in Elyza's. But then, her hair was nothing compared to those thick curls, which Emily knew would hold their perfect shape throughout the evening.

Charles was looking at Elyza with undisguised admiration, and suddenly Emily knew the comfortable visit she had enjoyed with him in the garden meant nothing at all. Gentlemen could complain about how much time ladies spent on their toilette, but there wasn't a man alive who didn't appreciate the results.

They had barely gathered in the drawing room when the guests began to arrive. "Lord and Lady Livingstone," intoned the butler, "and—"

"Lord Beddington," chorused Emily and Elyza in amazement.

"What the devil is he doing here?" demanded Charles.

"I suppose he is visiting the Livingstones," said Emily.

A slow smile grew on Elyza's face. "How delightful," she said.

Introductions were made and the company drifted into little groups. Lord Beddington joined Charles and the Vane sisters, and was quick to express his delight in seeing the ladies again.

"What a coincidence you should be visiting in the same neighborhood as we," said Elyza.

Beddington grinned. "Yes, isn't it?" He looked at Emily, a teasing light in his eyes. "Truth to tell, Miss Vane," he said to Elyza, "I could not resist the temptation to see how your sister did with her prospective in-laws."

"That was very kind of you," said Emily.

"Kind?" he countered. "Please don't weigh me down with such an honorable motive. My reasons were strictly selfish. I had hoped by now you two should find you didn't suit. That would leave the field clear for me."

Charles's frown showed he found no humor in this, and Emily blushed. Elyza looked momentarily insulted, then casually cast her gaze about the room as if the conversation was of no interest whatsoever to her.

The butler returned to announce the arrival of more guests. Even without his help, the Vane sisters would have known the newcomers to be the Bromwells, for little Betty, herself, was with them.

Oh, dear, thought Emily. She is exceedingly plump, poor thing. Elyza was looking with scorn on the girl, and Emily resolved then and there to give Miss Bromwell every gesture of kindness she possibly could.

Smiling, Elyza leaned over to her sister. "Do you see how she looks at Charles?" she whispered behind her fan. "Poor Emily. Here is more competition for you."

The teasing smile then froze on Elyza's face and her

eyes widened. Emily followed her gaze, wondering what could have turned her sister to stone. Then her eyes, too, widened, for entering the room in the Bromwells' wake were two young men. The first man was quite ordinary looking, with a pleasant but unremarkable face. But his companion was an Adonis.

Captain Fawley! Gwendolyn had not exaggerated in her description. Fawley's hair glistened as gold as Elyza's, and the shape of his nose and mouth were as perfect as the overall shape of his face. His chin was strong, and when he smiled, Emily saw straight, white teeth. She could find no flaw in his figure, either. His shoulders were broad, his waist and hips slim, and the fine leg he displayed she was sure owed nothing to padding.

The Adonis caught sight of Elyza and the carefree smile on his face turned to one of awe. Leaving his friend, he hurried over to them, begging Charles not to lose a moment in introducing him to the two glorious creatures who graced his house.

Emily couldn't help but smile at this bit of truth stretching. There was only one glorious creature present, and it was with great effort that the captain tore his eyes away from her to greet Emily.

Elyza was being oddly affected by the young man, blushing and stammering over her words, and Emily found this unusual problem truly amazing.

"It would appear your sister has finally met her match," murmured Beddington to Emily as Elyza and the captain drifted apart from the group.

Miss Bromwell and her brother joined them in time to hear the earl's comment. "Fawley has that affect on ladies," said Miss Bromwell dismissively. "Will you introduce us to your guests, Charles? Or, at least the one who is left. I am sure I shan't like either of them for they are both too pretty by far."

Charles chuckled at this and made the introductions.

"You are both such slight things!" exclaimed Miss Bromwell. "How ever do you manage when caught outdoors in a strong wind?" Emily giggled at this and Miss Bromwell went on, "It is a good thing you met me, for on stormy days, I shall be able to keep you safe. Just cling to me and you shan't blow away, for I am a veritable tree trunk. And if you should ever forget your parasol when we are out, do feel free to stand behind me. I shall cast a shadow large enough to protect you from the sun." Emily's face showed her amazement at such outrageous statements, and Miss Bromwell patted her arm and said, "I am a quiz, I know. Long ago I realized those of us who cannot make our way by beauty must develop other methods of being noticed. So I decided to be eccentric, and I find I rather like it."

And Emily found she rather liked Miss Bromwell. She was not displeased when she found herself seated next to that remarkable lady at dinner. Elyza, she noticed, was seated next to Captain Fawley, and barely touching any of the food that was served.

Miss Bromwell followed her gaze. "Every female succumbs to Fawley's charms at first. But don't worry. After they learn he hasn't a feather to fly with, they come to their senses."

No money? Mama would never approve Fawley as a suitor for Elyza, then. Poor Elyza. She would be heartbroken. A smile grew on Emily's face. How delightful!

Chapter Eleven

Emily quickly repented of her wicked thought. It would be no more than Elyza deserved if she were to fall hopelessly in love with Captain Fawley and then find she could not have him, but it would be horrible, too. It was a terrible thing when circumstances conspired against love.

Emily managed to catch Charles alone for a moment when the company made their way to the Grand Saloon for dancing. "Tell me of Captain Fawley," she said. "Is it true he has no money?"

"Hardly a farthing," said Charles. "He has been hanging out for a rich wife these past two years. Almost snagged Betty, but she has too much sense to fall for a pretty face. By the bye, what do you think of Betty?"

Emily forced her thoughts away from the problem of Elyza and Captain Fawley. "I like her very much," she said.

"I thought you would," said Charles. "She is a good sort, slap up to the nines. Even if she is big as a horse."

Emily frowned. "Why must gentlemen always be so concerned with a lady's looks?" she grumbled.

Charles scratched his head. "I don't know why a man

likes a pretty woman. I don't even know what makes a man think one woman pretty and another one ugly, well, except for the obvious things like a squint or a face like a horse. I only know that some women I look at and want to—" He stopped himself. "Emily, this ain't a proper conversation."

"I suppose not," said Emily regretfully. "But I should like to know. Love is a strange thing."

"I suppose it is," agreed Charles.

Once assembled in the large room, the young people took to the floor for dancing while Mrs. Bromwell, a lively woman with a face like a lump of bread dough, took to the pianoforte. She attacked the keys with as much verve as the dancers put into their dancing, and the other members of her generation settled down to tap their toes and watch.

"A lovely girl, your son's intended," said Lady Livingstone to Lady Fairwood.

"She seems quite sweet," admitted the viscountess, remembering her daughter's account of the jam incident in the nursery.

"If she is anything like her mother, I imagine she is," said Lady Livingstone.

"You knew the child's mother?"

Lady Livingstone nodded. "Emily Harrison was a sweet-natured little thing. I always thought she could have done better than Vane, but he was a kind man, and they seemed happy enough." Lady Livingstone shook her head. "This second wife is very different from Emily, I must say."

"What became of the first wife?" asked Lady Fairwood.

Lady Livingstone spread out her hands and shrugged.

"It is a common enough story. The poor thing died in childbirth."

"She did not . . . go mad?"

"Mad! My heavens, no. She was as sane as you or I. Whatever gave you such a queer idea?"

Lady Fairwood looked thoughtfully across the room at Elyza, who was smiling up at Captain Fawley. "Just a silly rumor I heard somewhere," she said.

After an hour of playing the pianoforte, Mrs. Bromwell declared her hands were worn to the bone and pronounced the music at an end, and no amount of cajolery could induce her to play even so much as a snatch of another song. The guests repaired to the drawing room for conversation.

"Are you enjoying meeting our neighbors and friends?" Charles asked Emily as they made their way down the hall.

"Very much," she said.

Charles lowered his voice. "I am sorry Beddington is among the guests. I don't know why that rascally fellow must keep popping his head up all the time."

"I suppose that happens in society," said Emily. "One is always running into the same people."

"I should like to run into him," muttered Charles. "With my curricle."

Emily giggled. But she did wonder what cause Charles had to take Beddington in such dislike. After all, it was not Charles's sister who had been lured down the Dark Walk. If anyone should hold a grudge against him, it should be herself. Of course, Charles was in love with Elyza, she concluded. Naturally he would not like Lord Beddington, for he would consider him a rival.

She heard her stepsister laugh and turned to see her walking on Captain Fawley's arm. There, she thought, was a rival to be feared more than Beddington, for Elyza had never looked at the earl the way she was looking at the captain.

The evening came to a close and the guests pronounced it delightful and made their exit, Captain Fawley casting one final adoring look at Elyza before going out the door.

Mrs. Vane was in raptures. Such delightful people! And Lord Beddington wasn't so very horrid after all. He had sat and conversed with her most pleasantly for a full ten minutes before allowing himself to be coaxed into leaving her side to take Edward's place in the dance. Perhaps Elyza should encourage him. But Captain Fawley was also a very personable young man. Of course, he was not titled, but so long as he had a respectable income. . . . What? Captain Fawley had very little income? "Well, then he won't do at all," she told her daughter.

Elyza said nothing, but a mulish look settled on her lovely face and Emily found herself feeling uneasy as she made her way to bed. If the captain was even half as headstrong as Elyza. . . . Here was trouble brewing in the pot if ever she'd seen it.

The following day at luncheon, Gwendolyn mourned having missed the party so very greatly that her brother suggested a picnic to cheer her up. "After all, who will care if she tags along on a picnic with people she has known most of her life," he told his mother.

"I suppose so," said Lady Fairwood. "But mind you, you must be responsible, Charles, and do not allow your sister to behave in an unladylike fashion."

"Mama!" cried Gwendolyn, stung. "When have I ever?"

Lady Fairwood smiled on her daughter. "Never, my love," she said. "You are a good girl."

"Ah, yes," put in Mrs. Vane, "it is such a comfort when one has good daughters." She, too, looked fondly on her daughters, her smile resting on Elyza.

Lady Fairwood said nothing, leaving the doting mama in ignorance of a certain young lady's naughty tale about madness in the family.

"Well, then," said Charles. "Whom shall we take along with us?"

"Betty and Edward," said Gwendolyn without hesitation. "They are like brother and sister to us," she explained to Emily, "and an outing would not be half so fun if they weren't along."

"Very well," said Charles. "I suppose that means we must invite Fawley as well, as he is staying with Edward."

Gwendolyn's face took on a dreamy look. "Oh, yes," she agreed.

Emily stole a look at her sister and noticed Elyza was wearing a disinterested look and a delicate blush on her face.

"Very well," said Charles. "We'll just send over a note and have them meet us tomorrow at two."

"I shall go ask Cook to make us some special treats to put in the hamper," said Gwendolyn, jumping up.

"Tell her to cook up plenty of chicken," called Charles as his sister skipped out the door.

"Yes, and if Betty is to come along, you had best have Cook make extra seed cake, for I know how fond she is of it," added Lady Fairwood. "Such a dear girl," she continued to Mrs. Vane. "She practically grew up under our roof. Her mama and I had fond hopes that she and Charles might make a match of it when they grew up."

Charles rolled his eyes.

Mrs. Vane looked less than pleased with this little speech. "Ah, but children will lead their own lives," she put in with a forced smile.

Lady Fairwood smiled graciously at Emily. "Yes," she agreed. "And it is just as well. Of course, much as we love Betty, we can see why Charles chose Emily for his bride."

Emily stole a look at Charles, who looked apologetically at her and shrugged. "That is very kind of you," she said, feeling suddenly self-conscious. "I am sure I don't deserve your son's affections," she added, thinking of the circumstances of Charles's proposal and feeling her sister's cynical gaze on her.

"Nonsense," said the viscountess kindly. "You seem a sweet, sensible young woman, and I am sure Charles will be very happy with you. And little Phillip positively worships you. Of course, I would be less than honest if I did not say we were all a little concerned when first we heard the news of our son's engagement. But his father had a long talk with him when he came down to visit and assured me afterward that he was sure Charles had made an excellent choice. And having met you, I must say I agree."

Emily felt her eyes prickle with the threat of tears. "My Lady is too kind," she murmured. What would her future mother-in-law think of her if she knew Emily had not only tricked her son into offering marriage, but now had cast aside all her noble intentions to set him free?

Charles sat next to her, scratching his head, obviously at a loss for what to say or do.

"Charles, dear," said his fond mama, "why don't you take Emily for a walk in the garden?"

"Oh, yes, of course," stammered Charles. "Come on Emily and I shall pick you some more lilacs."

"Oh, Charles, I am so sorry," Emily blurted as soon as they were safely away from the house.

"Sorry? For what?"

"Oh, you know. For all the embarrassing things your mother was saying. Really, I thought I would sink."

"She did not say anything all that horrible," said Charles. "Only that she likes you. And you ain't all that hard to like," he added. Emily smiled on him, and he cleared his throat and changed the subject. "Well, we have tomorrow taken care of. What shall we do today?"

"We could pay a visit to your little brother," suggested Emily.

"Not the whole afternoon," said Charles firmly. "I shall take you to see him before dinner, if you like."

"Very well," agreed Emily. "What would you like to do?"

Charles shrugged. "Oh, I don't know. Would you and your sister care to drive to Chipping Campden? It ain't far from here."

"That sounds a wonderful idea," said Emily.

Elyza was approached about the outing and agreed that a carriage ride to Chipping Campden would be just the thing. "I should like to purchase a new fan at any rate," she said.

Emily turned to Gwendolyn. "Would you care to come with us?" she offered.

"Would you mind terribly?" asked Gwendolyn, all eager shyness.

"Of course not," said Emily kindly, and Elyza gave a small smile. "Really," she said to her stepsister later as they made their way to their rooms to fetch shawls and bonnets. "Must you invite that child everywhere?"

"She is hardly a child," replied Emily. "She is, after all, only a year younger than you."

"She is not yet out and she is a child," said Elyza. "And she tires me with her constant gushing and fawning."

"She is Charles's sister," said Emily. "And if you do not wish her company, I suggest you remain behind."

"And, pray, what should I do here?" demanded Elyza.

"You may do whatever you like," said Emily. She stepped into her room and shut the door, ending the conversation.

Chipping Campden was a town inserted in a small fold of a valley along the edge of the Cotswold Hills. Its location had made it charming. Wool money had made it prosperous.

Its Church of St. James was the greatest communal gesture of the town and the first place where Charles felt obliged to take his guests. Built in the late fifteenth century, it was well worth visiting, but Elyza grew restive after a very short time, urging them to move on to the shops.

So they climbed back into the carriage and were driven down High Street. "It isn't much," observed Elyza.

"Oh, it ain't so bad," said Charles cheerfully. "Granted, it ain't London, but the inn has a tolerable ale."

Tolerable ale was apparently not important to Elyza. She wrinkled her pretty nose and pronounced the town boring. "Just another old country village," she said scornfully.

"Oh, it really is very nice," said Gwendolyn earnestly. "Charles, can we not go inside the Lygon Arms and have a pot of tea?"

The others assented and they entered the inn. Nothing there was fine enough for Elyza, who, since her come out, held up London as a standard by which everything must be measured. The room in which they were served was dowdy, the tea inferior. "And my cup is cracked," she observed.

"Here, now. We cannot have that," said Charles nobly, and signalled the proprietor to inform him that he was serving his guests with cracked china.

Much ado was made of this scandal, the innkeeper bowing and scraping as if Charles had brought Princess Charlotte, herself, in for tea, and within a few moments Elyza sat drinking from a new cup.

"Is that better?" asked her sister with sweet sarcasm.

"It will do," said Elyza.

"Well," said Charles heartily. "Another cake anyone?"

"Surely you jest," said Elyza.

"Something is wrong with the cakes?" guessed Charles in a strained voice.

Elyza laid a hand on his arm. "Dear Charles. I am sure it is not your fault that the cakes are dry."

Gwendolyn looked at her cake in surprise. "Why, I never noticed before," she said. "But now that you mention it, Elyza, I do believe they are a little dry."

"Perhaps we should start for home," suggested Emily.

"An excellent idea," agreed Charles in the voice of a man who was heartily fed up.

Elyza was her most charming on the drive home, making sheep's eyes at Charles and flattering him at every opportunity, coaxing him back into good humor. And the livelier Elyza became, the more quiet Emily grew. She felt like a cow at a horse race. Where was the sense in even trying to compete? What woman could compare with the beautiful Elyza Vane when she set her mind to being pleasing?

A stranger seeing the party return to Fairhaven would have thought Charles engaged to Miss Elyza Vane rather than Emily, for it was Elyza who took his arm and chattered gaily as they made their way inside the house, and Emily who followed behind with Gwendolyn.

Emily sighed as she entered her bedroom to change her gown. If she had come to Fairhaven alone, perhaps she would have been able to win some measure of affection from Charles, but with her stepsister bewitching him at every turn what chance had she? It was utterly hopeless, and she had been a fool to ever think she could win him away from Elyza. She cast aside her resolution to fight for him like a worn out slipper. She would set him free tomorrow. She could pick a quarrel with him at the picnic. Then he would be free to court Elyza. Another sigh escaped her, a sigh of resignation. Ah, well. At least that way Elyza would be safe from Captain Fawley.

Remembering her resolution to see little Phillip, she went along to the nursery, deciding to wait and change her gown after she had played with him. To her surprise, she found Charles there, and a startled, "Oh!" escaped her.

Charles looked happy to see her. "I say, Emily, you are a sport," he said.

"We did plan to come visit Phillip this afternoon," she said.

"I thought you would be too tired after our outing. Your sister said she was going to rest."

My sister expended a great deal of energy flirting, thought Emily sourly. No wonder she is tired.

"Charles is going to play war with me," said Phillip, pointing to the little metal soldiers lined up in rows on the floor.

"I see," said Emily. "May I watch?"

Phillip nodded solemnly and plopped down on the floor in front of his soldiers. Charles stretched out opposite him and moved a figure on horseback. "How did you enjoy Chipping Campden?" he asked casually.

"I thought it a charming town," said Emily.

Charles looked pleased. "Did you?" He sobered. "Your sister did not."

"My sister is easily bored," said Emily.

"There you are!" called a voice from the door. In walked Elyza in a fresh, pink muslin gown, looking like a newly bloomed rose. Charles jumped up. "Elyza. What are you doing here?"

"Looking for someone to entertain me." She pouted. "I am bored."

"You may play soldiers with us," offered Phillip.

Elyza merely laughed. "I should very much like to learn to play billiards," she told Charles in an intimate voice.

"Very well. Billiards it is!" declared Charles, jumping up.

"But Charles," protested Phillip.

"Now, tadpole," said Charles, rumpling the boy's hair. "I have to entertain our guests. I will come back up later and play war with you. I promise."

Phillip's lower lip trembled. "I was playing with you first," he said.

"Yes, but your brother must entertain his guests," said

Elyza. She smiled up at Charles. "It is one of those painful duties of a host."

"It won't be painful," Charles assured her.

Emily found this interplay more than she could bear. "Excuse me," she said, rising from her seat and hurrying toward the door.

"Emily," called Charles, "don't you want to play with us?"

She shook her head, not turning around. "I must change for dinner," she called over her shoulder and fled the room.

The evening was lustreless for Emily. She felt as though she were shrinking smaller and smaller with each passing moment. Soon she would disappear from sight altogether, and no one would miss her, for Elyza shone brightly enough for the two of them.

It was with a heavy heart that Emily went to bed that night. The picnic on the morrow would be no picnic for her, but merely fresh torture.

Gray skies came the following morning to forbid a picnic, spitting rain off and on throughout the day. Elyza was restive and hard to entertain, not being able to settle in to stitching with the other ladies, and even boring of billiards. And as she was not a great reader, not even Gwendolyn's offering of her favorite book from the Minerva Press could console Elyza for the lost picnic.

The rest of the week proved equally gray, and Elyza pronounced herself thoroughly bored. "I wish we hadn't left London," she complained, looking out the window.

"Elyza," scolded her mama. "Whatever will Lady Fairwood think?"

Elyza blushed, realizing her error. "I am afraid you will think me a very rude guest," she said. "The rain always gives me a megrim."

"Perhaps I should have cook brew you a tisane," suggested Lady Fairwood.

"That is very good of you," said Elyza meekly. She sighed. "If only we might see the sun. I know I would feel ever so much better."

The sun didn't rush to Elyza's rescue, but fate provided an even better cure—visitors, in the form of Edward Bromwell and Captain Fawley, who had braved the wet and ridden over to pay a call.

Elyza came to life, her tisane cooling and forgotten. "Oh, we are saved!" she declared. "I was about to perish with boredom."

"I am afraid two old women such as ourselves are sad entertainment for young people," said Mrs. Vane, smiling at the viscountess as if they were dear, old friends. "Mr. Bromwell, do come sit by my Elyza and cheer her up, for the rain has given her the megrim."

It was not Mr. Bromwell who took a seat next to Elyza on the drawing room sofa, however, but the penurious Captain Fawley. Mrs. Vane frowned and her sewing scissors fell to the floor. "Oh, dear!" she exclaimed. "I have dropped my scissors. Perhaps Captain Fawley would be so good as to fetch them for me."

The captain obliged. "Thank you," said Mrs. Vane. "Do sit next to me and tell me how you are enjoying your visit to Gloucestershire. And Mr. Bromwell, you may sit over there next to Elyza." Mrs. Vane smiled, having arranged the seating to suit herself.

But her victory was short lived, for Gwendolyn entered the room a few moments later. The gentlemen stood to greet her and when everyone reseated themselves, Captain Fawley had managed, once more, to secure a place next to Elyza.

The visitors left after half an hour, but their short stay

had been tonic enough to put Elyza in good spirits once again.

Captain Fawley, also, seemed to be in good spirits, and his friend teased him about it as they rode back home. "I wonder what can have brought such a smile to your face," mused Edward.

"She is the most glorious creature I have ever seen," confessed Fawley. "I wonder how she is situated."

"Well, she is probably no heiress," said Edward. "But she cannot be hopelessly poor. The Trevors would never align themselves with paupers, I am sure."

Captain Fawley smiled. "I am a happy man," he announced.

The weather remained determined to spoil all picnic plans clear through Sunday, giving Elyza little entertainment. Seeing Captain Fawley when the Trevors attended church, her stepsister noticed, put her in a better humor than any entertainment Charles had been able to provide for her during their time indoors at Fairhaven.

By the end of the day the clouds had drifted away, and the following morning the sun returned in all its glory to Gloucestershire. A footman was sent to the Bromwells to summon them to meet the Trevor party at the appointed picnic spot at two o'clock.

The picnickers set out, followed by a carriage containing two hampers filled with every imaginable delicacy, from preserved crab apples to pheasant and champagne, another hamper containing fine crystal and dishes, and a snowy white linen cloth to set them on, and the proper number of servants to lay out the contents of all three hampers.

The balmy temperature and gentle breeze pronounced that June hovered just around the corner. A June wedding thought Emily miserably. There would, most likely, be a June wedding, but she wouldn't be the bride.

So caught up was she in her miserable thoughts that she barely noticed when the carriages arrived at the picnic spot, and only Elyza's squeal of delight brought her back to her present surroundings. A stream ran by the Trevor land on its way to the Severn, flanked by lush, green banks and shady trees.

Elyza declared it a perfect picnic spot, and, once down from the carriage, she ran to the edge of the bank to inspect the stream. Captain Fawley followed her, catching her when she leaned too far over the stream and almost fell in. She gave a little shriek and giggle as he gallantly pulled her to safety, and the smile she flashed at him had felled lesser men.

The look he gave her in return was one Emily knew she would have given anything to have from Charles.

"It looks like a match to me," said Miss Bromwell, who had come to stand by her side.

"He is a fortune hunter," said Emily. "We have no money to speak of."

"Perhaps our captain will find he does not need as much money to live on as he once thought he did," suggested Miss Bromwell. "He and your sister could make a match of it, and Charles would be cured of his madness."

Emily felt her face growing red. "I am afraid I don't understand you," she stammered.

"I am sorry," said Miss Bromwell. "I do have a way of putting my foot in it. I speak where I shouldn't. But, pray, don't take offense. I think you are just the bride for Charles, and I think, eventually, he will see that."

Emily watched Charles, who had rushed to join the couple and now was making an unwanted third of himself. "I think we shall find we do not suit before the day is out," she predicted.

Miss Bromwell laid a hand on her shoulder. "Don't do something rash. Fate will prove your friend if you wait. I am sure of it." She took Emily's arm and walked her to a blanket that had just been laid out by a footman. "You did bring your sketching pad, did you not? Shall we capture the moment?"

Emily had no desire to capture the painful moment, but she pulled out her sketch pad and began to draw, hoping it would take her mind off her stepsister's antics. Edward Bromwell and Gwendolyn joined them on the blanket and Edward made idle conversation as the ladies drew. Emily forced herself to smile and reply when necessary, but like naughty children, her thoughts kept running away to the trio walking by the stream.

At last the food was all laid out. "We found a boat," announced Elyza, as the three joined the sketchers to fill their plates. "And Charles has promised that after we eat, we shall go out in it."

"Not I," announced Edward Bromwell. "I am sure all that rocking about would not agree with this fine champagne."

"Nor I," said his sister. "I should, most likely, sink the boat."

"Nonsense, Betty," said Charles. "It is a very sturdy boat."

But Betty would not be persuaded to leave the shore.

"Will no one go out with us?" demanded Charles. "Gwendolyn?" His sister timidly shook her head and he turned to Emily. "Emily! Surely you will wish to brave the stream."

Emily had no desire to be part of her stepsister's intimate little group. She opened her mouth to refuse, but before she could say anything Miss Bromwell answered for her.

"Of course, she will. And I shall sketch the event."

"I knew you wouldn't fail us," said Charles, giving Emily an approving smile.

"Well," said Captain Fawley to Charles. "Suppose we go and untie the thing."

"Right-o," said Charles cheerfully, and the two men bounded off to fetch the boat.

"You needn't go out on the boat if you don't wish to," Elyza said to Emily.

"Of course she wishes to," said Miss Bromwell in a forceful voice. "Why shouldn't she?"

Faced with a personality as strong as her own, Elyza backed down. "I am sure I don't know," she said pettishly. "I simply thought she might not care to."

Miss Bromwell's strength on her behalf had imbued Emily with new determination. "I think I am a good enough sailor to survive a boating on a stream," she said, and Gwendolyn looked at her with admiration.

Captain Fawley ran up to them and bowed low. "Your ship awaits, fair ladies," he announced.

Elyza giggled and allowed him to take her hand and help her up. He kindly assisted Emily up from the blanket, also, then offering an arm to each sister, escorted them to the bank, Gwendolyn, Miss Bromwell, and Edward following.

Charles was already in the boat, waiting to hand the ladies in. Emily got in first, the boat rocking as she stepped into it. "Oh!" she gasped, but Charles put a steadying hand on her arm.

"It will rock a little. Just bend down and grab both sides of the boat. You may take that seat in the bow."

He assisted Emily into her seat, and she looked

around her, smiling, enjoying the sensation of being afloat. "This is rather nice," she announced, and the Bromwells applauded her bravery.

Elyza was next. "Oh, dear," she cried as the boat wobbled at her entrance. She grabbed Charles in a fearful grip.

"Don't be afraid," he said. "I have you. You may sit right here."

He moved and the boat wobbled. Elyza gasped. "Perhaps we should not do this," she said. "I don't know how to swim. If we sink I will drown."

"We shan't sink," Charles assured her. "And even if we did, you wouldn't drown in six feet of water."

"But I would get wet. My gown would be ruined."

"We shall keep you safe," said Captain Fawley gallantly.

Elyza sank nervously onto a seat.

"We're off," called Charles, sitting down, as Fawley shoved an oar against the bank and propelled them out into the middle of the stream.

The others waved to them, calling, "Good-bye, good-bye!"

"Don't forget to write when you arrive safely," added Edward with a laugh.

Elyza began to relax. "This is quite pleasant," she said, looking around. She unfurled her parasol and set it over her shoulder, giving it a twirl.

A perfect picture, thought Emily, and wished they would fall into the stream. It would be worth getting wet just to see her sister with her perfect locks dripping in her face.

As if sent by Emily's good fairy, a fat bumble bee buzzed heavily in front of Elyza. She let out a squeak and jumped and the boat rocked.

"Elyza, you must sit still," cautioned Charles.

"A bee!" cried Elyza. "I detest bees! I swell all up when I am stung."

The bee droned by her ear and she let out another cry and jumped, shaking her head. She swatted at the bee with her hand.

"Just hold still," commanded Charles, rising. "I shall shoo it away."

"Here, I have it," said Fawley, half rising.

Heedless of Charles, Elyza was twisting and turning, and the boat was now rocking dangerously. Dodging a swat, the poor insect bounced off her neck and she lept up with a screech.

Emily watched as her secret wish came true before her eyes.

Off balance, Elyza pitched sideways with a yowl. Conscience and long habit made Emily move to save her sister at the same time that Captain Fawley leaned over in an attempt to catch her. Charles alone could not compensate for three people determined to tip them, and Elyza went into the stream with a splash as the boat tipped, sending the others in after her.

The stream proved to be just deep enough that the ladies could not stand with their heads above water. It took only a second for Elyza to realize this. "Glurkle!" she screamed. Her sister reached out a hand and grabbed her by the hair as her head disappeared under the water, and when Elyza came back up her face wore a look of pain and anger as well as fear.

Charles grabbed her and hauled her toward shore, and Captain Fawley gallantly took Emily in tow. They made their way out of the stream with Edward and Miss Bromwell's laughter ringing in their ears.

But Elyza saw no humor in the incident. She was

moaning as if she had been delivered a mortal blow. "My gown! It is ruined. And my hair!" She turned on Charles. "How could you have let us tip like that?"

"I?" protested Charles. "If you had sat still in the first place, we should have been fine."

"If I had sat still in the first place, I should have been stung to death," snapped Elyza.

"We are all safe now," said Emily gently.

Elyza turned on her sister. "No thanks to you," she said, pointing an accusing finger.

"Elyza, I am sorry—" began Emily.

"Sorry, indeed!" cried Elyza hysterically. "Sorry you deliberately tried to pull every hair from my head?"

"I was trying to keep you from drowning," protested Emily, pardonably exasperated. "Though heaven knows why."

Elyza burst into tears. "What a wicked thing to say! I shall tell Mama. Oh, I am going to catch my death!"

Charles had grabbed a blanket from the footman, who had come running to the rescue. He wrapped it around Elyza's shoulders.

"It is about time," she informed him.

"There now, it is all over," cooed Captain Fawley, coming to her side and leading her off. "Let us find something to dry your hair."

"I want to go home," she wailed.

Charles looked after her in disgust and shook his head. Never had he seen such a display. He turned his attention to Emily, who was accepting a blanket from a servant. The material of her gown was plastered to her body and every curve and valley stood out as plainly as if she wore nothing. His eyes widened and he swallowed hard. It was with great effort that he pulled his gaze away from the exciting little buds at the end of those high, full breasts.

Emily had seen his eyes on her breasts and blushed a deep scarlet as she pulled the blanket around her.

With an equally red face, Charles grabbed another blanket from the footman and draped that over her as well, hoping by this action to atone for his ungentlemanly stare. "I am sorry about this," he said.

"It is not your fault," she told him. "And it was fun." She shrugged. "Until Elyza fell in."

Charles frowned as a sudden realization dawned on him. "Things have a way of going sour when she is along," he observed.

Emily knew not what to say to this. She should defend her sister. But what Charles said was correct.

Charles didn't wait for her to reply. "Come," he said, putting an arm around her. "We had best get you home before you take a chill."

While the servants packed the hampers, Charles gently led Emily to the carriage, settling her on the seat as if she were a valuable piece of statuary in need of careful packing.

Edward and Miss Bromwell came to the carriage to bid them farewell. "I am sorry our outing ended so abruptly," said Miss Bromwell. "And I sincerely hope no one takes a cold from your spill, but truth to tell it was the most amusing spectacle I have seen in ages."

Emily smiled back at her. "It was all very silly," she agreed. "I hope we will be able to picnic again together before my family leaves Fairhaven."

"I am sure we will be seeing much of each other," said Miss Bromwell encouragingly.

Not once I have set Charles free, thought Emily sadly.

The captain arrived with Elyza and handed her tenderly up into the carriage. She took a seat opposite Emily, and with a toss of the head, averted her gaze from her "wicked" stepsister.

Little Phillip was out cavorting on the lawns when the carriage, with its soggy passengers, rolled up the long drive. As they came into sight, he gave a whoop and raced them to the front steps. "Why are you all wet?" he asked Elyza as she alighted from the carriage, still bemoaning the state of her hair, her gown, and her nerves to one and all. She brushed by him without answering. He tried again. "Why is everyone wet?" he demanded.

"We went for a swim," said Emily.

Phillip regarded her blanket encased form. "With your clothes on? That seems funny."

"Yes, it does, doesn't it?" replied Emily. "In fact, it was very funny." She patted Phillip on the head and followed Elyza into the house.

Phillip trailed in after them, watching wide-eyed as Elyza once more took center stage, informing her mother that she was nearly stung to death by a bee and then was pitched into an ice cold stream. "It was terrible! I almost drowned. And Emily"—here she looked accusingly at her sister—"nearly pulled every hair from my head."

Mrs. Vane gasped. "Emily!"

"I was trying to keep her from drowning!" protested Emily.

"In six feet of water? No one can drown in six feet of water. At least that is what Charles said before he let me fall in," said Elyza scornfully. She held out the sodden muslin of her gown. "My new gown is ruined," she finished on a wail.

"It was all an accident," put in Charles.

"My, my," tutted Mrs. Vane. "Elyza, you will catch a chill for certain. We must get you to bed immediately." She called over her shoulder, "You, too, Emily. Get those wet clothes off this very second before you become ill."

"Yes, Mama," said Emily meekly and followed the other two women up the stairs.

"Oh, dear," fretted Lady Fairwood. "Charles. How could you have been so thoughtless as to let our guests fall into the stream?"

Charles looked highly insulted by this accusation. "It was all her fault we fell in. I tried my level best to keep Elyza in the boat, but she insisted on thrashing about. If she had sat still we'd have all come back dry as toast."

"She is a big baby," pronounced Phillip.

Charles sighed a long sigh. "You are right, Phillip," he said with a shake of the head. "She is a big baby. And a big nuisance."

"Charles, dear, you are dripping all over the floor," said his mother. "You had best go change, also. I know men have stronger constitutions than ladies, but still, one should not take chances. I would hate you to take a chill."

Charles made his way to his bedroom, his boots squishing uncomfortably all the way. These were his favorite boots—Hoby's best, and they were ruined. To hear Elyza carry on, one would think she was the only one with nice clothes. He remembered the scene Elyza had made at the stream and shuddered. She had actually scolded him. Him! As if it were his fault they'd been pitched into the stream. And to give poor old Emily such a bear garden jaw when all she'd done was try to keep Elyza from drowning. . . .

Emily. A sudden vision of her breasts molded by wet muslin sprang to mind. Miss Emily Vane had a fine figure. What would it feel like to kiss her, to hold that pleasingly curved body close to his? Charles shook his head as if to dislodge such thoughts. How could he be thinking like that about Emily when it was Elyza he wanted? He did want Elyza still. Didn't he?

Foster helped her mistress change out of her wet clothes. After a hot bath, she patted Emily's hair dry and restyled it and put her mistress into a fresh gown. Feeling considerably refreshed, Emily decided to venture down to the drawing room. She had no desire to lay about in bed when she felt perfectly fine. As she made her way down the hallway, she heard raised voices coming from Elyza's bedroom. She tapped lightly and entered the room to find her stepsister and stepmama angrily facing each other. "Mama, Elyza, what is wrong?"

"Oh, it is too horrible," cried Elyza, throwing herself down on the bed.

"It is nothing of the kind," said Mrs. Vane sternly. "I have just been telling Elyza about the wonderful news I had from your father, something to cheer her after her ordeal."

"A marriage proposal from Lord Lardness wonderful news? He is as large as Miss Bromwell! And he wears a corset. I have heard it creak when he's bowed over my hand."

"You see?" said Mrs. Vane to Emily. "This is the kind of gratitude I get for bringing you girls to London, for sacrificing, never thinking of myself." She returned her attention to Elyza. "Lord Lardness is titled and as rich as Croesus."

"I don't care. I shan't marry him," announced Elyza.

A martial light gleamed in Mrs. Vane's eyes. "You most certainly shall. The season is as good as at an end and this is the first decent proposal you have had, for all the men you've had dangling after you. I shall not endure the humiliation of having to go another season in search of a husband for you, young lady. You will take this offer and be glad of it."

"I shan't!" cried Elyza.

Mrs. Vane's face turned an angry red. "You shall and there's an end to it. I am going to write your papa first thing in the morning and tell him to accept the gentleman's offer. We will return to London right after the ball."

Mrs. Vane stalked from the room and Elyza glared at her departing mother.

Emily thought it best to leave Elyza also. As she followed her mother out, she heard her sister mutter, "We shall just see whom I marry."

Emily bit her lip. Her stepmama had left the room like a conqueror, but her stepsister's words gave Emily the uneasy feeling that the battle was far from over.

Chapter Twelve

The Bromwells and Captain Fawley called the next afternoon to see how the Vane ladies fared after their fall in the stream. After biscuits had been consumed, washed down by sherry for the gentlemen and ratafia for the ladies, Lady Fairwood suggested the young people might enjoy a game of croquet on the lawn.

Servants were dispatched to fetch the croquet set and set up the wickets. While they did so, the young people ambled about the garden, admiring the statuary and the various shrubs and flowers. Emily watched nervously as Elyza and the captain separated themselves from the others. "I don't like this," she said to Charles in a low voice. "I am sure my sister is up to something."

"Our garden is hardly the Dark Walk," said Charles reassuringly. "I am sure she will be safe enough with Fawley."

"No. That is not what I meant. I think she is concocting some plan."

"What makes you think that?" asked Charles.

"Elyza has received a proposal of marriage," Emily announced. She looked worriedly at Charles. "I hope that news does not distress you too greatly."

Charles was amazed to realize that it didn't. "If that don't beat the dutch!" he declared. "I should feel heart-broken, but I don't."

Hope came to life in Emily's bosom once more, and she suddenly found she felt like skipping down the gravel path.

"Who has offered for your sister?" asked Charles.

"Lord Lardness. Do you know him?"

"Ha!" crowed Charles. "That fat, old dandy. I certainly do. Even blindfolded I should know when Lardness is in a room simply by listening for the sound of his corset." Charles sobered. "No wonder you are worried. Elyza won't have him."

"So she told my mama," said Emily. "But Mama says she will, and she has by now already written to Papa to accept the offer. I am afraid Elyza plans to do something rash."

"We must act with haste," Elyza was saying to Fawley. "For the ball is nearly upon us, and the day after we leave for London."

"We shall fly tomorrow," said the captain. "Edward will loan me his carriage. Bring your maid and slip out as soon as everyone has retired for the night. I shall wait at the end of the drive." He looked at Elyza in concern. "I wish I could come to the front steps for you. I am afraid it will be most frightening for you to come down that long drive in the dark of night."

"I shan't be afraid," said Elyza stoutly. "For you will be waiting for me."

"Brave creature," said the captain, and kissed her hand reverently. He looked quickly over his shoulder.

"We should join the others before anyone suspects we are planning an elopement."

"Oh, yes," agreed Elyza nervously, and let him lead her over to the Bromwells.

Emily watched her sister carefully as they all played croquet. Elyza seemed distracted. What was she thinking about? What had she and Captain Fawley been planning? There was only one thing a lady and gentleman could plan that would end with the gentleman kissing her hand, then looking over his shoulder. There was only one plan that could leave a lady so distracted. But when would they do it? That was the question.

Elyza's appetite seemed to fail her that evening. She ate little dinner, and when the supper tray arrived at ten-thirty, it brought nothing that could tempt her. While her appetite could not compare with Miss Bromwell's, Elyza had never been one to deprive herself.

There could be only one reason for her stepsister's lack of appetite, Emily concluded, and that was nerves. And since very few things made Elyza nervous, she had to be contemplating elopement this very night. Elyza patted a yawn, and now her sister was sure she was up to something, for Elyza was never tired before midnight.

"Ah, my poor, tired girl," said Mrs. Vane. "It must be this fresh, country air, making you sleepy. I vow, it certainly does affect me. I have not slept so well since the season began. The air in London is most unhealthy."

"There is no place like the country," agreed Lord Fairwood, and Emily thought it must be the first time she had ever heard the viscount agree with something her mother said.

"Ah, but polite society makes the city bearable," put in Mrs Vane.

Elyza yawned again.

"My dear child," said her mama. "Perhaps you had best retire. You look dead on your feet."

"Yes, I think I shall," said Elyza. "I hope everyone will forgive me for running away so early," she said politely.

"Of course we shall," said Lady Fairwood. "In fact, I must confess I feel a little weary, myself. Perhaps I shall retire also."

"It is all this work you are being put to on our behalf," said Mrs. Vane, rising along with Lady Fairwood. "So much fuss, a ball. I should have forbid your going to such trouble on our account."

Emily was sure Lady Fairwood was remembering how eagerly Mrs. Vane had pounced on the suggestion of a ball and, not for the first time, sent up a silent prayer that her stepmama would catch a cold and lose her voice.

The ladies all sought their beds early. The gentlemen stayed up longer, retiring to the blue saloon to shoot some billiards.

Although it was their first time alone together since the Vane family had descended on Fairhaven, Lord Fairwood did not bring up the subject of his son's engagement. And this was something for which Charles was heartily thankful, for he no longer knew what to think about his engagement, himself. He supposed he and Emily should end the pretense, but there no longer seemed an urgent need to do so. He no longer had any desire to be leg-shackled to Elyza, even if she was the most beautiful female in all of England. She was also the biggest nuisance.

"You seem preoccupied tonight," observed his father.

"Sir?" Charles asked, recalling his thoughts back to the same room as the rest of him.

Lord Fairwood repeated himself. "Are our guests proving to be a handful?"

"One of them is," muttered Charles.

The viscount smiled but said nothing more.

Father and son played one last game, then bid each other goodnight. The servants locked the doors and retired to their own quarters, the butler leaving a brace of candles standing on the table in the downstairs hallway for Lord Fairwood, who often was wakeful in the night and came downstairs to the library in search of a good book.

Emily sat fully clothed in her room, her door ajar a crack, listening for the sound of stealthy footsteps passing by. She was nearly ready to give up and call Foster from her cot in the dressing room to attend her when she heard a sound. She crept to the door and peered out. So! She had been right. Elyza had an assignation.

She let Elyza and her abigail get all the way down the hall and down two landings to the front door before coming out of her room, a cloak hastily thrown over her shoulders. They were already out the front door by the time she came down the stairs, and she wondered if, perhaps, she should have stopped Elyza right there in the hallway. It would have been embarrassing to be overheard and caught, but if she let Elyza get away, it would be more than embarrassing; it would be scandalous.

Emily opened the door and saw her stepsister and her maid disappearing down the drive. She hurried after them.

* * *

"I'm scared," whispered the abigail.

"Don't be a ninny!" snapped Elyza. "Nothing will happen to you here on the drive. Now, hurry!" And she, herself, picked up her pace.

Elyza saw no carriage when she reached the end of the drive and at first her spirits sank. But then she remembered she had told Captain Fawley that the household never went to bed before one in the morning. It had been not quite twelve-thirty when she left her room. Half an hour to wait in the cold. Elyza shivered.

"Where is he?" whispered her maid.

"Hush! He will be here soon." The sound of horses's hooves proved Elyza right, and she rushed out onto the road to see two horsemen approach. Captain Fawley and Mr. Bromwell! But where was the carriage? Surely the captain did not expect her to ride on horseback all the way to Scotland! The two riders came closer, and Elyza realized they were not the captain and Mr. Bromwell. She drew back behind the laurel hedge, pulling her maid with her.

Lord Beddington had seen the two women on the road. "It would appear we interrupt an assignation," he observed to Lord Livingstone.

"Well, well," said Lord Livingstone. "I suppose, as it is one of Fairwood's guests, we had best stop it."

"I suppose," agreed the earl, and nudged his horse into a canter.

Elyza stood next to her maid behind the hedge, listening to the strangers' approach and holding her breath. If they could just be quiet, surely the riders would go on by. She bit her lip to keep from crying out as the horses slowed down. Her maid burst into tears, and Elyza hissed an angry, "Shush," at her.

Too late. One horse came around the hedge, and there, looking bigger than life itself, was her old admirer. "Lord Beddington!" she gasped.

"What a pleasant surprise, Miss Vane," he countered. "Out for a stroll?"

"Yes," she managed. "I could not sleep."

"And you were lonely, so you decided to take your maid with you," suggested Beddington.

"Yes," she said slowly. "But I think I am feeling sleepy now, so I will bid you goodnight, my Lord."

"Allow me to escort you back to the house," offered the earl, hopping down from his horse.

"Please don't trouble yourself. It is most unnecessary," said Elyza.

"Oh, but it is," said the earl, undaunted. "One never knows whom one may encounter this time of night. I should hate to see someone make off with you."

Elyza bit her lip, and the earl stood watching her. She seemed to come to a decision at last, saying, "It is very kind of you, my Lord."

They strolled slowly up the drive, Elyza chattering of what a fine night it was—how lovely the moon, how warm the air . . .

"A perfect night for travelling," observed the earl.

"I suppose it is," agreed Elyza calmly, and the earl's mouth twitched. She might have been able to maintain her charade all the way to the front steps if it hadn't been for the sight of her sister coming down the drive. "Emily!" she cried. Her eyes narrowed. "You were following me!" she accused.

"Miss Vane, what a pleasant surprise," said Beddington. "Were you feeling the need of some exercise also?"

"Er, I could not sleep," said Emily.

"It must be the full moon," said the earl. "Your sister could not sleep, either. I found her lingering at the end of the drive. Perhaps that is a late night snack her maid carries in the portmanteau."

Elyza clamped her lips together in an angry line, and flounced on up the drive.

"I cannot thank you enough for your kindness," Emily said to the earl.

He bowed. "It was no trouble, really. Livingstone and I were on our way home and passing by."

"Fortunate for us," said Emily. "We are in your debt. I hope someday I may find a way to repay it."

Beddington smiled down at her. "You may name your firstborn child after me," he said and Emily blushed. He bowed over her hand, mounted his horse, and left her to hurry after her sister.

By the time Emily caught up with Elyza, she was mounting the front steps. "How dare you!" she called back over her shoulder.

"Don't make it look as if I am the guilty one," retorted Emily. "What were you thinking of?"

"My future! And, as usual, you have quite ruined it." Elyza jerked the door open and stomped inside.

"I!" hissed Emily, following after, the poor maid scuttling along behind her.

"Yes, you!"

Elyza's voice was rising dangerously, and Emily took the brace of candles from the table at the foot of the stairs and ushered Elyza into the library, saying, "We will have this out once and for all." She shut the door in the maid's face, put the candles on the desk, and turned to face her recalcitrant stepsister. "I have done nothing to ruin your life. You have been managing to do that quite well all by yourself."

"I! I suppose it was I who ruined my chance to marry Fawley tonight."

"An elopement?" Emily looked scornfully at her sister. "That seems to be all men want to do with you, run away. Are you not good enough to marry decently?"

Elyza's eyes widened in shock then narrowed to slits. With a squeal, she rushed her sister, hands raised, nails ready to claw.

Emily was as thoroughly angry as her sister, and she met her with raised hands of her own. With much screeching and yowling, the two girls bounced off the desk, each looking for a clawhold and heedless of the teetering candles. Elyza found a clump of Emily's hair and yanked, and Emily cried out in pain. From outside the door, Elyza's maid called to them, but they fought on, unhearing. Arms flew, along with words, and objects were knocked every which way as the sisters careened around the room.

Neither noticed when the candles tipped over. It was only the acrid smell of smoke that brought Emily to a halt. She turned in time to see the top of Lord Fairwood's desk aflame. "Fire!" she cried.

Elyza screamed and ran for the door. Emily grabbed a nearby vase and dumped its contents onto the desk, sending up a billow of black smoke.

"Here now, what's this!" cried a voice from the door. With Charles right behind, Lord Fairwood rushed into the room, nearly colliding with Elyza.

Elyza was set firmly aside, and a heavy velvet drape yanked from the window and thrown over the remains of the fire, smothering it.

Lord Fairwood turned from his charred desk, his bushy brows meeting in an angry V. "What has happened here?" he demanded.

"I am so sorry," said Emily. "We were quarreling and—"

"And I am afraid my sister got angry and managed to knock over the candles," put in Elyza. "We are truly sorry," she said humbly, as Emily stared at her, gapemouthed.

Lord Fairwood looked sternly at the sisters. "There is little harm done," he said. "I suggest you both find your beds, which is what you should have done an hour ago."

At that moment Lady Fairwood rushed into the room, a vision in a pale pink wrapper, with her hair in curl papers. She clutched at her heart. "Oh, my gracious!" she gasped.

"Just a little accident, my dear," said her husband, taking her arm and leading her from the room. "But all is fine now. You may go back to bed and not worry."

"Not worry! Oh, it smells absolutely dreadful. The whole house will smell of smoke by morning."

"We will open the windows and air the room," said her husband comfortingly. "All will be well."

"But look at your desk," lamented Lady Fairwood. "And the drapes. There is no help for it. We shall have to redo this room as well as the rest of the house." Her husband looked at her as if she had just announced her intention to cut off his head. She took his arm and led him from the room. "Now, Harold, I know you did not wish the library done, but the smell of smoke will linger, I assure you, no matter how much we clean the carpet and wash the walls. I have a wonderful idea. . . ."

The room fell into silence as the viscount and his wife drifted up the stairs to the third landing to find their rooms. Charles looked from one sister to another. The two young ladies stood for a moment, each glaring at the other, then Elyza raised her chin and marched from the room. Emily sighed and made to follow her.

Charles caught her arm. "What happened tonight?" he asked.

"Elyza tried to elope with Captain Fawley," said Emily in a tired voice. "Fortunately, Lord Beddington and Lord Livingstone were passing by and found her."

Beddington again! How he hated to be indebted to that rogue. But how had Emily happened to be up when Beddington brought her sister back? "Did you know Elyza was gone?" Charles asked.

"I had followed her down the drive," confessed Emily. She rubbed a hand over her tired eyes. "I should have let them go. At least, then your library would have suffered no harm." She gave Charles a tired smile. "I hope your father does not have an aversion to Chinese dragons."

Charles grinned. "You are an amazing woman, Emily Vane," he said, and suddenly realized how true that was.

Emily blushed and preceded him out of the room.

Mrs. Vane managed to sleep through the entire incident, but she heard of it first thing the following morning. From Elyza. Emily was immediately summoned to her mother's room. "What horrible thing have you done?" demanded Mrs. Vane as soon as Emily was inside the bedroom door.

"I?" echoed Emily. Oh, it was too much! "I merely tried to stop your daughter from eloping with Captain Fawley."

"I was not eloping with anyone!" cried Elyza.

"Then why was your maid with you?" retorted Emily.

"We were taking a walk," said Elyza. She turned to

her mother. "You see how it is, Mama? I told you she would say wicked things to protect herself."

"Oh, and you have said nothing wicked?"

Mrs. Vane clapped her hands together. "Silence!" she commanded. "You have both behaved abominably. How I shall be able to look Lady Fairwood in the eye this morning, I have no idea. I can only say I am relieved we will be heading back to London in a few days. I shall, of course, have to offer to pay for the damages you have both caused, and what your papa will say to that I cannot imagine. What must the family think of us? Oh, I shan't leave my room all day. I feel a terrible megrim coming on."

Mrs. Vane was pacing now, and Emily nervously shifted her weight from one foot to the other. She had the beginnings of a headache, herself, for she had slept little the night before, going over the quarrel with her sister and the resulting horror again and again.

A tap on the door stopped Mrs. Vane in midpace and she called a nervous, "Come in." In stepped Lady Fairwood, herself, and Mrs. Vane rushed to her and took her hand. "Oh, my dear Lady Fairwood! How can I ever apologize for what my wicked daughters have done!"

"Please do not berate yourself," began Lady Fairwood.

"Not berate myself? I am nearly prostrate with grief! I shall never be able to hold my head up again. Your poor library. Oh, what must you think of us?"

"I must think that your daughters suffered an unfortunate accident, that is all," said Lady Fairwood graciously.

At this kindness Mrs. Vane burst into vociferous tears.

"You must not cry, so," pleaded the viscountess. "There is no harm done, really. In fact, I am most grateful to your daughters." Mrs. Vane looked at her in amazement and she smiled and said, "I have been wanting this age to get my hands on the library. It is sorely in need of redecorating. My husband has resisted most stubbornly. But now, you see, he has no choice. So things have come to a most satisfying end."

"Kind creature," said Mrs. Vane tremulously.

"Now, do come sit in the morning parlor with me and let us discuss our children's wedding."

"Oh, dear. The wedding. I quite forgot," said Mrs. Vane in distracted accents. "First the offer from Lord Lardness and the need to leave for London, then that horrible incident last night. Oh, my! It quite oversets me even to make mention of it."

"Then, pray, do not," said Lady Fairwood kindly. "We shall sit in the morning parlor and drink a dish of tea."

Charles found the ladies gathered in the small room his mother had referred to as the morning room. "Ah, Charles," called his mother. "We are setting a date for your wedding. Does the end of June suit you?"

Emily looked guiltily at Charles, who was looking thoughtful. "Yes, it does," he said, and smiled at her in a way that set her heart fluttering. Oh, they must end this charade soon! For Charles was becoming too good at playing his part, and if he looked at her like that even once more, she knew she could not bear it.

"We have decided to use St. James Church at Chipping Campden," continued Lady Fairwood, "then we will return here for the wedding breakfast."

At that moment, Captain Fawley and Edward were

announced, and the making of plans for Charles's and Emily's wedding was temporarily abandoned.

The visitors had not sat long before Edward suggested a stroll in the gardens.

Everyone agreed a walk outside in the sunshine would be just the thing, Mrs. Vane following her daughters with determination. "Oh, Mrs. Vane, will you bear me company for a few moments?" said Edward Bromwell with a smile. Mrs. Vane had had no choice but to graciously nod her head and walk with him. And Edward Bromwell, it seemed, was determined to show Mrs. Vane the most lovely roses in bloom—roses which lay in quite the opposite direction as the captain and Elyza were walking.

Emily had hoped to keep an eye on her errant sister, but Gwendolyn had latched onto her and was now dawdling along at a most annoying slow pace. Emily craned her neck to see around the hedge that set off the formal gardens, where her stepsister and the captain had disappeared.

Charles had been about to chase after them and send his sister away so he might have a few moments alone with Emily when his mother laid a hand on his arm. "Charles, dear, a word with you, if I may?"

"Of course," he said politely.

Lady Fairwood came right to the point. "I do hope you did not mind my offering to have the wedding here in Gloucestershire. I wouldn't for the world hurt Emily's feelings, but I thought perhaps, our home might be a little nicer for a wedding. And this way we might have some control over who is invited to the wedding breakfast, for heaven knows what sort of toadying people that stepmother of hers would wish to include if it were in her home."

"An excellent idea, Mother," agreed Charles.

Lady Fairwood sighed. "Unfortunately, it means we shall have to bear with having the sister under our roof yet one more time, but I suppose we can manage. If we still have a roof by the time they have left," she added, and her son smiled.

"I suppose Father told you what I related to him about last night."

"Yes," said his mother, "and I must say it does not surprise me." She patted her son's arm. "I congratulate you on your good taste, dearest."

Charles raised a questioning eyebrow.

"Most young men would have chosen the lovely face. You had the wisdom to look beyond that, and I am sure you will be most happy."

Charles felt an uncomfortable flush on his face. How right his mother was. And how wrong! He had, indeed, chosen the lovely face. And the wrong girl. It was only by mistake that he found himself engaged to the right one. And that engagement was a sham.

"Well, now, dear, that is all I wished to say. Why don't you go find Emily and enjoy a nice visit with her?" his mama concluded and turned him loose.

Find Emily. An excellent idea! What a fool he had been! How long had he been in love with Emily, anyway? No wonder he so strongly disliked Beddington. Beddington! Why the devil was the fellow hanging about the neighborhood, anyway? Probably because he still wanted Emily, and was just waiting to take her for himself the minute she broke off her engagement. Charles set his jaw in determination. He had to talk to Emily as soon as possible, before she did something he would regret.

* * *

"We must try again," said Captain Fawley to Elyza.

"There is not much time left," she said. "We leave the very day after the ball."

"Then we shall elope from the ball," said Fawley. "I think Edward will still stand our friend, but if not, I shall rent a carriage. Have your maid waiting at the end of the drive with your portmanteau and we shall fly as soon as the supper is ended."

"Hello," called a cheery voice.

Elyza turned to see her stepsister and Gwendolyn approaching. A frown crossed her face before she put on her most charming smile. "Emily, Gwendolyn! We were just talking about the ball!"

"Were you?" replied Emily in airy accents, her gaze penetrating.

Elyza turned her back on her stepsister, choosing to sniff a rose. "Only smell! It is too wonderful."

Gwendolyn and Emily both obligingly bent their heads to the roses. Emily sneezed.

"Bless you," said Gwendolyn, and Emily sneezed again.

"Perhaps you should go inside," suggested Elyza. "You might be taking a chill!"

"Nonsense," said her sister. "It is a perfectly warm day." She sneezed again and pulled her shawl around her shoulders.

"Oh, dear," said Gwendolyn, looking at her in concern. "Are you not feeling well? Perhaps we should go back inside."

"I am fine, I assure you," said Emily, determined not to leave the two lovers alone in spite of the fact that she was, indeed, feeling very poorly. The headache that had visited her earlier in the morning when she was with her stepmama and Elyza had never left her, and she did, indeed, feel chilled, in spite of the warm sunshine covering her shoulders.

At that moment Charles made his appearance. "Emily is not feeling well," Gwendolyn told him.

He looked at Emily in concern. "You do not look at all well," he informed her. "Allow me to escort you into the house."

"It is nothing, really," said Emily, and swayed. Charles put a steadying arm around her waist, and she found herself wishing she felt well enough to enjoy the comforting sensation more properly.

"If it is nothing," he said, "then you'll be right as rain in time for dinner. But if you are coming down with a summer cold, we had best get you to bed before you become too sick to attend the ball."

"Oh, Charles," she fretted as he led her into the house. "You must promise to keep an eye on Elyza for me."

"Yes, yes, I will," he said impatiently, brushing aside the subject of Elyza. "You really do look pale, Emily," he said earnestly.

Emily refused to be turned from the subject weighing so heavily on her mind. "I am sure they plan to try and elope again," she continued.

"What! Who would be so dunder-headed as to try and elope twice in one week?" scoffed Charles. Emily looked at him as if to say, need you ask? "Right," he said. "We'll keep a close watch on 'em."

"Thank you," murmured Emily.

Charles fell silent a moment. This was hardly the time to speak about marriage, when his betrothed was coming down with a cold, but if he put it off, what fresh disaster would befall them? And with Beddington stalking about ... "Er, Emily," he began. "I know this ain't the time to talk about our engagement, but—" Charles came to a sudden halt, unsure how to go on.

Emily bit her lip. "Yes, Charles," she said in a quiet voice.

"Oh, my dear, what is wrong?" cried Lady Fairwood, hurrying to meet them. "Are you unwell? Do you feel faint? I shall ring for a footman and we shall have you carried up to bed."

"Oh, no," protested Emily weakly. "I am not so ill as all that, but I must admit that I should like to lie down. I fear I am coming down with a cold."

Lady Fairwood took charge, tut-tutting over Emily, and helping her upstairs. Charles watched them go, feeling unneeded and unwanted. He went back out into the garden and wandered aimlessly up and down the gravel paths, kicking the little white pebbles with the toe of his boot. He wondered how soon Emily would be well and when he would ever get a chance to make her a proper proposal.

Chapter Thirteen

Emily spent most of the remaining days before the ball sick in bed. When she was finally well enough to leave her room, she spent her leisure hours sitting in the drawing room, visiting, always surrounded by others. Charles ground his teeth in frustration when he thought of the many times he'd had the opportunity to speak with Emily alone and hadn't known his heart. Now, when he truly wanted to declare himself, it seemed every member of his family and every neighbor for miles around was against him.

At last, on the day of the ball, he had an opportunity to speak with her, but her mind was not on him. "I am sure Elyza and the captain are going to do something tonight," she fretted. "Oh, Charles. How will we ever be able to keep watch over my sister with such a crowd of people milling about the house?"

"We will manage," said Charles. "Emily, there is something I have been meaning to speak with you about."

"Oh, there you are my dear!" exclaimed Mrs. Vane, bustling into the drawing room. "I think it is high time you went upstairs to rest. We don't want you worn to the bone and unable to enjoy the ball tonight, especially since it is in your honor."

"But I am not tired, really," protested Emily.

Mrs. Vane shook a playful finger at her. "I know what it is to be young and in love, but we must be practical. I am sure Charles wants you looking your best tonight. And there will be time enough to be together after you are married."

Emily gave Charles an apologetic look and allowed herself to be shepherded from the room.

The door shut, leaving him alone. He swore and punched a sofa cushion.

The ball to introduce the Trevors' many friends and extended family members to Charles's intended was a glittering affair. The Grand Saloon was a veritable jungle of hot house plants. A thousand tiny flames burned from candleabras, causing the jewels of the distinguished guests to wink and sparkle. Outside, the gardens were lit with Chinese lanterns, and guests strolled along the gravel paths to cool themselves and admire the floral wonders wrought by Lady Fairwood's gardener.

Inside, the musicians imported from Chipping Campden were playing a waltz, and Charles and Emily were enjoying themselves very much. "Do you remember our conversation the first time we met?" asked Charles.

Emily blushed. "I certainly do. And dancing with you is still like flying," she said, and lowered her eyes, embarrassed by her boldness.

"I am glad I mistook you for your sister at that masked ball," said Charles. "Else I might have never had the sense to ask you to dance."

Emily looked at Charles in amazement. "Why, Charles! What a nice thing to say!"

"I wasn't simply being nice," said Charles. "I meant it."

The music ended, and before he could say anything more, they were set upon by Edward and Betty Bromwell. "Wonderful crush," said Edward. "Er, Charles. Could I speak to you a moment?" Without waiting for an answer, he pulled Charles aside. "I thought I should tell you. I think Fawley means to make off with Miss Vane tonight."

So, Emily was right! "How do you know?" demanded Charles.

"Well, he asked about borrowing my carriage again. I must admit, I helped him the first time out. You know, love and all that. But I got to thinking it ain't quite right, much as I'd like to help the love birds. My parents would kick up a dust. So would yours. I told him he'd best rent one for himself. Quite understanding he was, too. Don't know why he thinks they need to elope. Nice fellow, Fawley."

"He ain't got a feather to fly with," said Charles in disgust. "That's why they need to elope. And besides, Elyza's mother already has another husband lined up for her. One Elyza don't want, from what I understand."

"That explains it," said Edward. "Too bad, really. Perhaps I should have loaned 'em a carriage."

"Thank God you did not," said Charles heartily. "When do they make their escape?"

Edward shrugged. "Don't have the fig of a notion. Sometime tonight."

Charles made a face. "Very helpful," he said.

Edward shrugged again.

"Well, go see what you can discover, then let me know."

"Right-o," said Edward cheerfully. "But I must say I think it a curst shame. Fawley really is the devil of a good man, and Miss Vane is so lovely. I think they'd make a bang-up pair."

"With hardly a cent between them," said Charles scornfully. "Oh, now here is supper being announced. See if you can get to Fawley before he and Elyza go off in a corner somewhere to eat."

Edward left to do Charles's bidding, and he returned to Emily, who looked up at him in concern.

"Is everything all right?" she asked.

"Oh, yes," he said airily and heartily wished both Elyza and Captain Fawley at the devil.

He tried to spot the pair among the milling crowd as he took Emily in to supper, but was unable to see them anywhere. Half an hour, six lobster patties, two ices and three cups of champagne punch later, Edward reported in. Charles set aside his fourth cup and leaned forward eagerly. "Well? What did he tell you?"

"Nothing," said Edward.

"Nothing!"

"Couldn't find him. It's such a bloody crush I am lucky I found you again."

Charles frowned. "What is it?" asked Emily nervously.

"They could be walking in the garden," suggested Edward.

And they could be halfway to Scotland, thought Charles irritably. Well, it was worth a try. He smiled at Emily, trying not to look as if anything were wrong. "Do you feel like some fresh air?" he asked.

Emily looked at him nervously. "They are gone," she guessed.

"We don't know that for sure," said Charles, trying to sound calm.

Emily was already wringing her hands.

"Here, now," cautioned Charles. "We must appear calm. If we don't, people will smell a scandal." He rose and offered her his hand. "Let's take a stroll."

Emily smiled weakly. "Yes, all right," she said, rising.

"I'll help you," said Edward. "But really, Miss Vane, you must not worry too much. Even if they have eloped. Fawley is a very good man. I can vouch for his character."

"If he has as much character as you say, he should not be attempting to elope with my sister," said Emily sternly and left a blushing Edward to follow them out into the gardens.

Once outside, they each agreed to try a different path. Charles flushed out two kissing middle-aged couples, and Edward encountered his own sister strolling with a portly admirer. Emily was nearly run over by a young lady running up the path with her hair in disarray. But no one found Elyza and Captain Fawley. Emily turned to Charles. "What shall we do?"

"Tell my father," said Charles.

Lord Fairwood was easy enough to find. He was in another room, playing cards with several of the older gentlemen. When pulled aside and told of the situation, he frowned. "Your sister seems determined to ruin herself," he informed Emily. "But I will not have her ruin this family's reputation, nor a ball given in honor of yourself and my son. We shall, of course, fetch her back. But not until our guests have departed."

Emily began to wring her hands afresh. "But we might not find them if we wait," she worried.

"And we might not find them if we don't," argued the viscount. "It may be that this Fawley fellow will take her to stay with friends to throw us off the scent." At this Emily's lower lip began to tremble. The viscount patted her shoulder comfortingly. "But," he continued, "if they are headed straight to Gretna, I assure you we will have them before this night is over, so there is no need to distress yourself. Either way, what will be will be, and we shall come about. Now, don't let your sister's foolishness destroy your ball." With that, the viscount commended Emily into his son's care and returned to his card game.

The evening seemed to stretch on and on for Emily, stretching her nerves equally tight. Once she even snapped at her stepmama, who offered her a windy diatribe in response, forcing her to humbly beg forgiveness, and flee to a quiet corner of the room.

"Are you feeling unwell?" asked a voice at her elbow.

She gave a start and turned to see Lord Beddington looking down at her. "Oh, my Lord. I am fine," she said in a wobbly voice.

"Yes, as is your fiancé," observed Beddington. "Have you quarrelled?"

Emily shook her head and blinked several times in an effort to hold back the tears.

From across the room, Charles had seen her talking to the earl and was now descending on them in a determined manner.

"No, it would appear you have not parted ways, for the whelp seems as possessive as ever," concluded the earl.

Charles was standing in front of them now, acknowledging the older man with a stiff bow. "Good evening, Lord Beddington," he said.

"Good evening, Trevor," said the earl easily. "I have not seen your future sister-in-law this past hour." Charles turned white at this, and Beddington said, "I see." He turned to Emily. "Will you excuse us, Miss Vane?" Without waiting for an answer, he put a friendly arm on Charles's shoulder and propelled him away from Emily. "I take it Miss Vane and the good captain have eloped."

Charles hated having to disclose his embarrassing predicament to the earl and his face showed it as he nodded.

"How long would you say they have been gone?" asked the earl.

"God knows," said Charles miserably. "We have been searching for them this past hour."

Beddington nodded. "I think it is time I took my leave. Perhaps I may encounter them going for a moonlight drive. If so, I shall be happy to escort them home." Charles stared dumbfounded at Beddington, and the earl smiled. "I have a great fondness for your bride-to-be," he said, "and would hate to see her embarrassed. She is worth ten of her sister, you know, and if you should find you, er, don't suit—"

"My Lord is, perhaps, referring to a certain unfortunate piece of information that got out earlier in the season," said Charles stiffly.

Beddington nodded.

"I am afraid I did make a mistake," admitted Charles. "But my biggest mistake was in not seeing the hand of providence in it. I hope to rectify that as soon as we have found Elyza."

Beddington smiled ruefully. "May I be the first to congratulate you?"

"I hope so," said Charles fervently.

Lord Beddington left and Charles returned to Emily. "He knows, doesn't he?" she said.

"Yes, but he is going to help us look for them." Charles took Emily's hand. "Don't worry, Emily. We shall find them."

"Oh, I hope so. I do wish this ball would end."

At last it did. The guests departed, all except those family members who had come to stay an extra day at Fairhaven. And as soon as they were safely seen to their beds, the searchers mobilized. Charles and then Edward, who had felt honor bound to return and offer his services, left on horseback. Lord Fairwood prepared to follow by carriage, the same carriage that would be used to bring home the prodigal daughter.

On being told of Elyza's flight, Mrs. Vane had promptly swooned, then come noisily back to life, insisting on accompanying the men. All Lady Fairwood's persuasive powers had been of no avail in convincing her to stay at home and wait for news of the eloping pair, but the viscount had decided her with only five words, "Madam, you shall not go." And with that he had left, sending Mrs. Vane into fresh hysterics.

Emily, herself, felt too numb for hysterics. Poor Charles. Poor Lord and Lady Fairwood. How glad they all would be to be rid of the pesty Vanes! As soon as they had returned with Elyza, she would break off her engagement with Charles. There would be no more putting it off. Her stepmama would be angry, of course, but at least she would still have one daughter engaged. If they could keep this escapade a secret.

* * *

Little Phillip was out playing on the lawn when Lord Fairwood's carriage returned to Fairhaven in the early afternoon the day after the fateful ball, Charles riding behind. With a whoop, the little boy raced across the lawn, his nurse struggling to keep up. He reached the front steps in time to see a tearful Elyza handed down from the carriage, followed by his father, looking very stern, indeed. Even Charles didn't look like his usual merry self. Phillip followed the adults inside the house, hoping for a show.

But there was nothing half so entertaining to be seen as there was the day the picnickers had fallen into the stream. Elyza was sent off to her room. His father scolded him for being under foot and handed him over to his nurse, who bore him back off to play outside.

After disposing of his small son, Lord Fairwood strode into the drawing room, to deal with Mrs. Vane, Charles following close behind. "We have found your daughter, madam," he announced.

"Oh, thank God," cried Mrs. Vane, jumping up. "I must go to her immediately."

The viscount held up a hand to halt her. "But first, allow me to inform you of the circumstances in which we found her."

"Oh, dear," whispered Mrs. Vane, sinking back down onto the sofa. Emily, who was also present, put a supporting arm around her shoulder.

"Your daughter had the misfortune to flee in a rented carriage, which broke an axle and landed her and her lover in a ditch, where they were obliged to stay until dawn."

Mrs. Vane let out a moan.

"Just so," said the viscount. "Lord Beddington found them, and stayed with them for propriety's sake, but the Kilbarnes happened upon the wreck and offered to take them up, and I am afraid Lady Kilbarne saw your daughter's portmanteau and will have drawn certain conclusions."

Mrs. Vane's moan increased in volume.

"I would suggest you return to London and start to plan your daughter's wedding to Captain Fawley immediately."

"Oh, dear, yes," said Mrs. Vane. "Oh, that foolish girl! She has whistled a fortune down the wind."

"Ah, yes, but she has chosen love," said Lady Fairwood comfortingly.

"One cannot eat love," snapped Mrs. Vane. "Come Emily. We must pack."

"Why not let Emily remain with us?" suggested Charles quickly.

"Yes, do," said Lady Fairwood. "I am sure you will have much on your mind, making arrangements for Elyza and her captain. Let us keep Emily another fortnight."

"So kind," murmured Mrs. Vane. "Oh, there is so much to do. So much. Now, Emily. I hope you may not be a bother to Lord and Lady Fairwood while I am gone."

"I shall try not to be," said Emily meekly, and Charles covered a laugh with a cough.

"Well," said Mrs. Vane briskly. "I must go pack. What Mr. Vane will think of all this I cannot imagine."

"He will, most likely, think himself well rid of a great many headaches," muttered Lord Fairwood as the door closed behind Mrs. Vane, and the others giggled.

Charles turned to Emily. "Would you care to walk in the garden?"

Emily's smile fell. The heart that had only a moment ago felt so light with Elyza's problems suddenly seemed made of lead. "Certainly," she said, and allowed Charles to lead her out the French doors and onto the lawn.

Once outside, she plunged into her rehearsed speech. "Charles, I would like you to know how sorry I am for all the trouble my family has caused you—"

"Hang your family!" declared Charles, and he grabbed Emily by the shoulders, pulled her to him and pressed his lips fiercely over hers.

When at last he released her, she looked at him in wide-eyed shock, trying to make sense of what had just happened.

"That was not at all how I meant to do it," he muttered, and taking her hand, he pulled her off to the garden and seated her on the same stone bench where only weeks before he had consoled her stepsister. "Emily, you must marry me," he said earnestly.

"Charles, you have been pretending too long," began Emily, unable to comprehend her great good fortune. "Have you forgotten you offered for me quite by accident?"

"And it was the luckiest accident I have ever had," said Charles. "Curse it all, Emily! I don't want your sister. I want you! Please don't cry off."

Emily stared at Charles. "Charles, can you really mean it?"

Charles tenderly gathered Emily in his arms and proceeded to show her exactly how much he did mean it. At last, a rustling in the bushes caused him to raise his head and look around. A look of irritation crossed his face. "What is it, Phillip?" he sighed.

Phillip crept out of his hiding place and proffered a small box. "I have something for Emily," he announced.

"Why Phillip, how sweet!" exclaimed Emily, and took the present. She lifted the lid and a small frog jumped out, causing her to let out a squeal as the frightened amphibian leapt to freedom.

"Phillip!" reprimanded Charles as Emily burst into laughter. "What kind of a thing is that to do to your new sister?"

Phillip hung his head, but Emily smiled. "I know exactly what kind of a thing that was to do," she said. "And I hope I have passed the test." She scrutinized Phillip's red face.

He nodded. "I am sorry, Emily," he mumbled. "I knew you wasn't like the pretty lady. I just wanted to be sure."

Charles took Emily's hand and kissed it. "I am sure," he said.

Shortly after Mrs. Vane returned home, a letter from Mr. Vane arrived for the Viscount Fairwood.

"I greatly regret the illness which prevented our meeting," wrote Mr. Vane, "but regret is hardly a strong enough word for what I felt on hearing of all the trouble my stepdaughter, Elyza, caused your family on her recent visit. I am forever in your debt for doing what a father should have been present to do, and can only hope that the fine wife my daughter Emily will make your son will atone for the terrible houseguest Elyza made."

"Very prettily said," observed Lady Fairwood, handing the letter back to her husband. "And seeing how happy Charles already is, I should say the child has more than made up for her sister's sins."

"I must agree," said the viscount. He paused. "It is not the match we would have chosen for him."

"Fate chose," said his wife gently.

The viscount patted his wife's hand. "Contrary to what the poets tell us, it would appear Fate is not always cruel," he observed.

The June sun beamed outside St. James Church at Chipping Campden. The families of both bride and groom sat scattered about the pews, watching as Charles and Emily exchanged their vows. Edward Bromwell stood as groomsman and Gwendolyn as bridesmaid.

The lovely Elyza was not present, as she was honeymooning with her new husband, and it might be said that no one missed her presence in the least. Even Mrs. Vane seemed too busy enjoying her moment of triumph to give much thought to anything else. She beamed up at the bride and dabbed at her eyes with a lace hanky.

Viscountess Fairwood did the same, and her husband smiled tolerantly at the pair at the front of the church. Mr. Vane was smiling also, and his smile was definitely that of a proud father.

As for the bride and groom, all agreed they made a fine pair, for what bride and groom do not? Emily wore an elaborate gown of white and silver, her veil held in place with a floral headdress of white roses. And the face she turned to Charles glowed with a radiance that transformed it from plain to lovely. Charles was resplendent in cream-colored satin breeches, a cream-colored waistcoat embroidered with roses, and a Clarence blue jacket.

As he smiled at his bride, no one present would have guessed this marriage to have come about by mistake.

For although the groom had acquired his bride by accident, the kiss he gave her to seal their vows was most purposeful.

Sheila Rabe welcomes letters from her readers.
Please write to her in care of:

Zebra Books
850 Third Avenue
New York, NY 10022